KING OF THE CARNIVAL

KING OF THE CARNIVAL

AND OTHER STORIES

WILLI CHEN

Published in Great Britain by Hansib Publications in 2006
First published in 1988 by Hansib Publications

Hansib Publications Limited
London & Hertfordshire, UK

Email: info@hansib-books.com
Website: www.hansib-books.com

ISBN 1 870518 12 8

Printed and bound by Butler and Tanner, Frome & London, UK

Acknowledgements

For

Fred, Mom, Jay, Jason, Gregson, Minton,
the CHEN family and to the memory of
my father JOHN CHEN.

Contents

Foreword

The story with which this collection opens establishes the attitude or stance from which nearly all the stories come. The narrating character is not exactly one of the villagers but he is intimate with them, and involved. He is familiar with them, but can neither take them for granted nor fail to be surprised by the things they do. He knows them well enough but is always finding out something new. He is learning.

Willi Chen's parents, John Chen (1906 – 1979) and Iris Chen came to Trinidad from the village of Tien Tsien in the Guandang Province of China. This is the first collection of stories by a Westindian writer of Chinese origin and in it we find Chen revealing his belonging to the new world his parents entered as aliens. At the same time, the stories show him exploring the levels and expanses of this meeting ground of cultures from Europe, Africa, India and China.

Willi Chen has been well-known as a painter in Trinidad and the Caribbean since the 1960s. He has also engaged in batik work, ceramics and metal enamelling. All these skills and interests are in evidence in the mural installed at Central Bank in Port of Spain with which Chen won the Central Bank of Trinidad and Tobago Sculpture Competition in 1986.

Chen combines these activities with running his own successful bakery (Wonderbread), and his own printing and packaging plant (Printex Converters) in Marabella near San Fernando in South Trinidad. He is a man who gets things done.

In 1981 this self-taught artist embarked upon another career, this time as a self-taught writer, winning at once first place in the Drama category in the Trinidad and Tobago National Cutltural Council Competition. Since then he has been prolific and versatile, winning prizes in the annual competition in the poetry and short story categories as well.

The first of his literary efforts to gain wide attention were the plays *Freedom Road* (1985) and *Tainted Blood* (1986). The former deals with life on an estate in the sugar belt during the 1950s, and focuses on the struggle with poverty and underprivilege of a family of Indian origin harassed by an overseer of African origin – one aspect of the Creole world impinging upon the still (in that period) closed but vulnerable world of the descendants of Indian indentures. Chen's short stories continue to explore and express, but in a more satisfying manner, the meeting of races and cultures in the sugar and agricultural lands of South and Central Trinidad where the author grew up.

The second well-known play *Tainted Blood* has a more contemporary setting and deals with the penetration of drugs and drug dealing at all levels of society and especially in this story, among the police. This topical piece shows Chen as practitioner of a comedy of violence, built out of the same violence that pervades the stories.

The present collection then, is a collection by a painter, dramaturge and man of affairs. They show some of the descriptive gusto of the painter and the 'new' writer taking delight in the discovery of words. There are sometimes weaknesses of conception and in structure that arise from an imagination quick to seize upon the vivid character, the startling event, always on the lookout for the exemplary story, but not always patient enough to await the discovery of the perfect form.

At the centre of the collection lie the Bastahall stories. Bastahall is a tiny village near Esperanza Estate in Couva, central Trinidad, inhabited mainly by descendants of indentured Indians who were brought to the Caribbean between 1838 and 1917 to replace the liberated Africans on the sugar plantations. This group of stories deals with the lives of Indian descendants and includes *The Stickfighter, The Girl from Bastahall* and *Lalloo's Wrath.* In *Lalloo's Wrath,* Chen makes use of the common occurrence of the wife's flight to the home of her parents after a beating or a quarrel (the husband is usually drunk). From this place of refuge she has to be persuaded to return by the promise of her now sober husband that it will not happen again. In Chen's story the soberness is mental, taking the form of a fear of loneliness and the persuasion is a non verbal eruption which is as effective as it is sudden and desperate. Lalloo takes an axe to the offending house that withholds his wife, with the terrified Dulcie reading the meanings of Lalloo's savage attack upon the object; "He was attacking the last stilt with the same savage fury of a madman, the crumbling, decaying boards collapsing in a heap over him, the dust rising in clouds. She rushed out of the yard at top speed, this time down the road from which she had come the night before. She did not look back."

In *The Girl from Bastahall,* Chen draws upon the familiar conflict between arranged marriages and a love match among the Indians, and upon the common belief about the Indians' dramatic tendency to suicide by gramoxone (herbicide in use among farmers) as a way of ending love complications. Here, an erring husband discovers with a devastating unexpectedness that he loves the wife whose body lies beside that of their child whom she had included in her depressed act of suicide. Chen's climax convinces us that the husband's suicide at this point is a logical and triumphant act of love.

Certain general features of the Bastahall community – the inter-connection of lives in a small community, strong emotions, and primitive rages and revenges are integral to the drama in *The Stickfighter*. This story exemplifies another socio-cultural characteristic of Chen's stories. Chen explores for spectacle, and uses a number of outstanding elements of the popular culture on the island as forms of authentic self-expression (for example stick-fighting, Carnival and cock-fighting). He draws from these sources heroic figures like Bogo the stickman and Moro the anancy-like game-cock trainer. It is clear that Chen is struggling in his stories towards expressing the ordinary heroism and the legendary qualities of the folk even while he is fascinated by the meeting of cultures which is a characteristic of his island society.

In the comic conclusion to *Assam's Iron Chest,* it is the Chinese 'victim' who proves to be the bigger thief, and in *No Pork, Cheese* as well as in the delightful *Trotters*, stories that draw upon the Muslim component in the Indian community, Chen writes with understanding and humour of the mine-field of taboos people must observe or seem to observe in his society. Where Chen allows his characters to talk, as in *Trotters*, the author's facility with dialect and his dramatic gifts release the work into a lightness and sureness that are sometimes lacking in the stories where narration and description predominate.

From its rural base and its cast of village characters, the collection broadens into the violent world of marijuana merchants *(The Killing of Sanchez)* and drug dealers *(Death at Coramandel)* and in *Caesar* Chen tells of the love and grief in an affair between an ex-patriate airline pilot and the Trinidadian woman whose love never gets a chance to prove itself because of the unspoken cultural tensions in the atmosphere they live in.

These are humane and well-observed stories whose strong passions and recurrent violence are balanced by the surprising strength of love and the capacity of decent feeling and good heartedness to overcome the petty and the prejudiced.

It is a pleasure to welcome a writer who is clearly beginning strongly.

Kenneth Ramchand
University of the West Indies
St Augustine.
Trinidad

The Stickfighter

When I took him down that afternoon amid the black flutter of wings darkening the branches overhead, the sun was almost down, but the heat was still there, trapped in the hollows that encircled the tree of death. There was no time to pause or to find the answers for all those questions that rushed into my brain: the squabbles, the unanswered letters and his long absence. All these answers were lost forever in the dampness of his brows and quieted by the pallor of death.

I touched his cold arm, turning him around where the noose had bitten sharply at the nape of his neck. I was struck by the blueness of his skin and its tautness, by the morbid puffing out of his eyelids and cheeks that could not contain the protruding tongue – I had seen enough. I eased the tension of the corpse as he swung back under the groan of the rope and our life time's friendship rallied in front of me just before I swung the cutlass, felling him onto soft ground.

Bastahall loomed in the distance, a dusty, arid maze, a scrabble of brown earth trampled by oxen. On my left, the sea of cane ended at the mangroves which receded seawards, where the vegetation was lush and green with the glut of herons, lily white. I had tied the cart at the nearby clumps of blacksage. The beast was still, not even moving to shake the flies off its rump, as if sensing the gravity of the situation, with the stench of death around us.

Rain fell that afternoon and mud clung to my boots in wet chunks. With petite marie sticking to my pants' fold and around my chest, I had difficulty getting the body onto the cart. I tied the hands together, then passed the rope around the body so that the arms remained together. The denim trousers were stiff with mud from the fields where he had worked.

When I first met him he was already in his thirties, gaunt, nothing extraordinary in his walk or speech. There was nothing startling enough to stir him. His was a world of peace and work. He spent his time in the shelter of the pens, caring for the animals and feeding them. He could have been well over six feet, but his lean figure lent him an air of pure grace. I knew he was strong in all his gentleness, but it was in the gayelle where he circled like a hawk on the hot sand, head tied, and the red end cloth of his stick fluttering in the breeze like a signal of death, that I saw in him special quality which made him a champion.

Those were Scottie's heydays, black and powerful, already renowned in the districts as an established stickman, who used to come down from Carolina to play in Couva, his stick pushed straight behind his back at his buttocks as if it were the natural position for keeping his weapon. He limped slightly, bending his right knee a little more quickly than he should, with a slight drag of his foot, almost in a slow crawl. But in the gayelle no one observed his peculiar gait, for when the stick was held poised with both hands, people looked at its whirring speed as it became alive.

Then there was 'Nation', that mulatto who grinned impishly under the barrage of blows, but who always retaliated with a speed and power that could break his opponent's stick in two. He was very swift, but Alphaeus was even more dangerous. He, too, came in search of battle down the mud paths from Chickland, head aloft, tied with the narrow strip of white cloth in fine style.

All the battles were fierce and colourful. Blood dripped on the sand, oozing from the broken heads. They continued long into the night as the kegs of mountain dew emptied and the drums boomed louder and louder around the bonfire. On those afternoons of gruelling pace, the strongest survived as they circled the hot sand under the blazing sun that parched their throats and broiled their sweating bodies.

It was strange that no one really knew his real name and no one ever bothered to find out. But everyone called him Bogo, even the smallest child, and they suspected it was only a nickname which he had brought with him when he first came into the village. Perhaps it was his quiet nature that impressed us, his ambling, carefree nonchalance, and the way the smoked-out cigarette butts hung from his half-closed lips, the long ash drooping precariously to the side whilst the smoke rings rose over his head in measured puffs.

Late one afternoon Bogo arrived from Esperanza village where he occupied a single room in the barracks, which stood adjoining others in rabbit-hutch fashion with the bland facade of cheap bricks. He looked happy, the straw hat took on a steep slant and the red parrot feather on it was colourful. He met us drinking beneath Latchun's shop. He knocked the ash off his cigarette and said "Boys, ah getting married."

"Doh make joke, man!" Ramlal said.

"Yes, man, ah going shack up with Indrani."

"Who you mean? Rajbool daughter-in-law?" I asked.

"Used to be, man. Ah taking over now," Bogo thumped his stick on the ground as Boyoon downed the glass of

Carupano rum and spat, missing the spittoon by a full two feet. I jumped off my stool.

Ramlal poured another drink and said, "Come man, Bogo. You mean to tell me dat you going take Indrani away from Sonnyboy, and they not even married three months yet?"

Bogo took off his straw hat and patted it, straightening the bright red parrot feather. He replied, "Dat girl getting real bad treatment and she don't have no family."

"How you come in this business?" I asked him.

"I come in this business because ah seeing advantage." He turned the hat around in his hand.

"Is true, Ramlal", Boyoon said. "Since dat girl come to live by, is endless horrors for she; licks like peas."

"What she do so bad?" Ramlal asked.

Boyoon continued, holding the glass of rum in his hand: "Well, boy. Ah hear is two time she does get licks; in the morning and in the evening, that is before he go to work and when he come back. One time she run away by she sister in Felicity. Dat is the only family she have."

"And why she don't stay there?" I asked him.

"Well, ah hear the sister and all have de same problem. She does get she share ah licks too. De only difference is she have children and she can't go no way," Boyoon continued.

"But, Bogo, you don't have no right wid she either and dat is husband and wife business," Ramlal interjected.

"Dat is true, Ram, but you going to wait till she dead before ah man do something. The man drunk everyday. He father have cattle and land. Dat doh mean he must beat the woman like that." Bogo said, still turning the hat in his hands as he patted the red feather.

"Do what you want, Bogo, but dis ting will bring trouble

and besides Sonnyboy not going to take this lying down. He bad like crab and not only that, he know more badjohns than you."

Bogo gave the hat one turn with his right hand, balancing its crown at the tip of the index finger of his left hand and raising his head he said, "Well, boy, anybody could be a badjohn and ah don make up me mind already; the girl coming by me. I have a old cot and she will stay as long as she want."

Then in one movement he tossed his hat into the air, in a wide arc. As it descended, Bogo shifted lithely, braced himself and then, rocking on the tip of his toes, moved his head as if wanting to dodge it. With arms outstretched for balance, he bent his knees the same way I saw him so many times before in the gayelle. Then he raised his shoulders and the hat fell plump on the crown of his head, with its peak turned backwards. He jumped, pulling his stick over our heads and with the same movement of his arm, swung it around and around until his hand became almost invisible. The stick climbed skywards with its end cloth trailing. For a moment we stood looking at Bogo standing slim and tall like some sign post in the yard. He moved once more. Slowly at first, like a cricketer in the field anticipating the ball in the air, shifting to the right, then to the left and suddenly he raised his right arm in a flash, and the plummetting stick appeared in his hand. Raising it once more he swung the stick, churning the air as it whirled at an astonishing speed. In a minute he was gone leaving us mesmerised by his dexterity.

One week passed and Indrani's move to Bogo's room on the sugar estate was the only incident that warranted any lengthy talk in the rumshops, or in the fields amongst women with their blackened faces where the sway of poignards would stop momentarily and their chatter take on new colour. The people thought about Bogo, a renegade and skulker, the ignoble penman, a labourer who found himself her keeper, her lover. To Sonnyboy, the spoilt son of the prominent village landlord, this state of affairs was a slap in the face; an insult to his prestige, discrediting his manhood.

It was no surprise then that Sonnyboy came up to the barracks one day with some of his friends and demanded that Indrani come home. It was evening time, when the last cane carts were rumbling home and the cane cutters walked behind, swinging their empty calabashes and crooksticks, their clothes blackened from the burnt cane ash.

Standing at the roadside near his Land Rover jeep, Sonnyboy called, "Indrani, you home? Ah come for you!"

The small group of men with him remained silent. There were three of them, one sitting on the bonnet of the jeep. Hearing no reply, he left the group and came into the yard. He encircled his mouth with his hands and called out in a half-demanding, half-pleading manner. In the darkness he hoped that the men standing around the jeep could not detect the urgent tone of his voice.

"Indrani, make up you mind, ah losing me patience. Indrani, ah not begging," he said. "If you don't come, it go be real war and tell Bogo he go be in it too."

Behind the fragile door, Indrani peeped through the crack and became frightened. She saw him in the yard. She hoped he would not come any closer to the gallery. He continued, "Indrani, answer or I go break down the door."

She gathered courage: "Ah not coming back and if you touch the door, Bogo go do for you."

"Oh is so? Well is me and you. Go tell Bogo is war. You hear? Is war!"

"Go away now, ah not coming back," she replied.

"Tell Bogo is fire today and we waiting by the marketplace for he." He shouted desperately in a louder tone so that his friends could hear him. "Tell he come with his pouistick. Is blood and sand. It go be licks and we go spread he out like rice on the ground, you hear?" he shouted angrily.

The Land Rover sped off in a cloud of dust.

The next day was market day. The women trekked from Bastahall, Springland and from as far as Indian Trail that went beyond remote Carolina. They came with oiled feet, dressed in their waterwashed tunics, unstarched orhnis, with glinting bangles and nose rings and with baskets under their arms, as they filtered into the marketplace and crowded the vendors who crouched behind stalls and squatted behind shallow trays of Indian sweet meats and market produce. Colourful clothes were displayed and bright bolts of cloth cascaded from carts. The hawkers peddled their wares with an open voice beneath the papery grace of whirling wind mills held shoulder high, colouring the wind.

Far from the hustle and chatter of bartering women was the gayelle, a small grass-fringed patch of earth that shimmered in the sun, the white sand soft and hot. Around its perimeter sat the drummers with busy hands, their naked legs wrapped tightly around the drums. It was here the men gathered to smoke ganja, as the stench of mountain dew soured their breaths and clouded their senses in wanton gaiety. It was here too they found action.

Bogo was standing, leaning against the watermelon shed one foot on the crossbar, as if to support the rickety structure. His hat angled and his cigarette dropped, accentuating the smirk on his lips. He waved an arm and soon we were deep in conversation.

"Boy Charlo, I must keep Indrani. I get to like the woman now, but I don't know what will happen."

"Well, you sure Sonnyboy will take her back?" I asked.

"That I don't know. You mean she have to go back for more licks, better she go back to she uncle," he said.

He could not disguise the tone of pity in his voice. His moistened eyes betrayed his feelings. With his arm over my shoulders, we walked into the open when the sudden outburst of voices assailed us in a frenzy. The voices were distinct in the crowded stalls.

"Bogo, they looking for you, Scottie and Ranny, and Victory...Nation and all. Sonnyboy bring them for you...is cut ass dey say."

"Better turn back," another voice said. I grabbed Bogo's arm, tugging at it and said, "We better really do that, Bogs. Is trouble up there. Let us go home, man."

But he just stood there, suddenly motionless, and the twinkle had gone from the brown of his eyes and in its place came the cold glint of steel. His whole body tensed, and I knew it was useless pleading with him, for the time had come, as Sonnyboy had promised.

The crowd gathered around the gayelle. Tar-chested, Scottie seemed blacker in the sun as he stood against the soft milkiness of clouds with the daubs of violet shadows beneath his brows, his lips, and flaring nostrils. He loomed even more terrible in the sunlight, a figure of doom bringing with him expertise and power, as he strutted on the sand, like some overgrown African doll with the strip of yellow around his head. He threw his stick on the ground in challenge, picked up sand in his hand, rubbed his wrists and forearms and flexed his fingers. Then he raised his 'bois' high over his head and shouted in defiance:

"Is Bogo, ah want, that mule-pen man. Where he?"

We stood in the shade; Bogo was silent as he leant on his stick.

"Where' the man wife, lover man?" Scottie bellowed.

I pulled Bogo's shirt sleeve again.

"You can't fight that man, Bogo. He go kill you."

"Never run from a man yet, Charlo."

Scottie exposed his mighty chest, reeled around in a circle to the pound of drumbeats, churning up the sand like a rhinoceros preparing to charge.

"Come, Bogo, is blood ah want. You afraid? Either you bring Indrani or play bois with me," Scottie shouted.

A chuckle rippled through the crowd. I saw Bogo straighten himself and I knew then that he was angry. He walked into the gayelle, stick in hand, a gaunt figure, wiry in his whip-like stance, his old straw hat pulled right over his eyes and the long cigarette drooping from the corner of his lips. He stood like some dry mora yard post with neither colour in his figure nor valour in his presence except for the one red parrot feather in his hat band. Scottie pranced up and down like the champion he had long proven himself to be, gallant, strong, warrior from the Carolina foothills, pride of his villages.

Bogo pulled his hat over his head to hide his eyes, and when he raised his stick, the red end cloth fluttered, the poui stick gleamed and the brass of the ring at the other end sparkled in the sun. Scottie approached him in the squatting position as he shook his weapon over his chest, clasping it with both hands, his massive thighs angled to support his gargantuan frame. The yellow strand of cloth lifted in the breeze behind his head, and someone at the back muttered, "That is stickman. He from Carolina and I never see his head bust yet."

"That the man Sonnyboy bring to beat Bogo?" another asked.

"That the killer. Watch how he foot, strong like iron."

No one saw the first blow, only the scuffle of moving feet as they lifted the sand in the wind, but Scottie had struck the first stroke, following up with four more in rapid succession. Then Bogo, cool, his eyes beneath the dim canopy of his old straw hat, shifted his tall frame to the left and parried the blows with little fuss. The drumming stopped, the crowd gasped. Scottie's face showed surprise and Bogo, standing erect, did nothing but pulled his hat over his head once more and the drummers pounded the goatskins again.

Now Bogo, tall in the sun, raised his head. His right leg trailed with the pants' fold loose on the sand, and he peeped from below that old straw hat once more, his eyes concealed, rolling like marbles within the dark confines, as if to verify the position of the moving target. The strip of yellow cloth swayed in the breeze and his own head bobbed and weaved to the drum beat.

Suddenly he exploded into action. Speed was the keynote of his attack. His slender poui came down with lightning force on Scottie's head, reddening the white sand around his feet as the thronging crowd, hoarse and sweaty, backed away in disbelief, as they saw their champion reel under the battering blows. Six times the limbering stick descended from the blue heavens, digging deeply on the same spot on the crown of his head until the white of Scottie's eyes shone, exuding cold terror and pain. The yellow strip on his head reddened to a deep scarlet.

A gentle wind rustled through the coconut trees but it failed to soothe Scottie's wounds and the drops of his own blood seemed larger and redder than jumbie beads in the sand. He knelt on the ground a pitiful sight, spattered with his own blood and his shirt in tatters. The crowd roared in disbelief. Scottie, the black giant from Carolina, was biting dust. Sonnyboy then turned to Victory.

Victory sprang out from the coconut shade, snarling. There was evidence of skill and experience in this man. A scar ran from the top of his head to his brows, over the eyelids down to his chin on the left of his face; his left eye never blinked. He pranced up and down with his 'bois' raised, smooth, brown and thick. Bogo stationed himself at the other end of the gayelle, still bobbing and weaving to the staccato of drumbeats, eyes still hidden beneath his hat and his pants' fold dragged over the sand. They circled and taunted each other – Bogo forever watchful – Victory, swarthy and muscular, sneaky in his feinting movements. The drummers struck up a note of frenzy. The crowds pushed; the men sang;

"Is you moustache we want, Hitler

Oi Oi Oi.

Is you moustache we want Hitler.

Hear what Chamberlain say?"

Sonnyboy bellowed, "Take him, Victory. Is he blood we want, not Hitler moustache."

There was a sudden rush and Victory, stooped so low that his grey stubble touched the ground, lifted himself like some leviathan out of the marsh, with hands upraised, and dug and dug again with his 'bois' into

Bogo's head.

Victory was savage in all his assaults. He crouched and bent his whole body from the waist sideways as he levelled his poui before him. Again he charged with terrific speed, coming with both hands clasped on his stick, leaping high into the air, before landing in the arena. His stick whirled and tore into Bogo, who by this time had withdrawn to the left. Bogo drew his 'bois' across his chest and, holding it vertically on the ground, received the full force of his opponent's blows. His stick vibrated under the strain, and one blow caught him on his waist, tearing his shirt.

Victory stepped back once more, both hands clasped his stick whilst he rested on his knees, as if taking stock of the situation, assessing the skill and the craft of this stickman. Who was he and where did he come from? Rising again he tiptoed to another attack, but Bogo advanced slowly, still gazing from beneath the shade of his straw hat, the pants' fold trailing on the sand. They angled again, Bogo moved up, shook his head to the beat of the drums. He paused, now turned to the right, then to the left, stalked his prey, spun his web. Victory turned to the left too, then Bogo jumped. He darted like lightening, the red end-cloth dived to the ground. The spot of brass dazzled, turned in a circle and crashed on Victory's head, tearing into his temple and behind his left ear. Blood splashed on the sand.

The crowd pressed forward, only to scatter when the fighters clashed in mid-air and the rattle of their sticks echoed through the coconut groves. Victory fired four times, one missed its mark. Bogo crouched, blocked twice and ducked from the last stroke. Then he levelled his 'bois' at Victory's head. The crowd moved nearer again seeing only the quick movements of his hands and the brass ring that circled over Victory's head like a bee diving to sting. A new fissure appeared on Victory's right temple and soon his whole head reddened in the sun.

He stumbled on the ground and his blood mixed with that of Scottie's, while Bogo stood like an obelisk, calmly swaying with the music of drumbeat, his eyes peering from beneath the rim of his straw hat. The drummers stopped. Bogo watched, not even acknowledging the chant from the crowd. Despising the lusty clamour for more blood he walked towards Victory, held his hand and lifted him up. He tore a strip out of his own shirt and bandaged the head wound, knotting it tightly at the back of Victory's head. Then putting his stick back in his hand calmly, he walked out of the gayelle.

I saw him pull that old straw hat over his head again as he disappeared into the crowd with the red parrot tail bright as ever. It was then that another challenging voice erupted from the other end of the gayelle as 'Nation', dressed in black silk and a scarf around his neck, jumped into the arena, hoarse from the war cries loud in his throat. But by then, Bogo had already gone.

That was the last I saw of Bogo for some time because I had moved into Charuma at the end of the Carnival season and, for once, avoided the hot black cane stalks for the cool of cacao and coffee. The hiatus proved no remedy for forgetting and the haunting memories of Ramlal and Boyoon, mountain dew and rhummy in the almond shade came in flashes before me.

Bogo remained on my mind. He visited me twice, after which he seemed to disappear. I wrote him two letters which were never answered. It was Boyoon's account of his whereabouts that troubled me. I met him at Jerningham Junction on the railway platform, about four months later.

The midday special train left me in Savonetta, a small outpost with a signal cabin, a solitary hut in the middle of peas and bodi beans. I jumped behind my knapsack, leapt over the oil-soaked railway sleepers and I was soon in Esperanza. I was confronted by padlock and crapaud timber scantlings set diagonally across the front door of Bogo's barrack room. Three hens picked at spilled rice in the yard; an overturned tub lay beneath a drooping clothes line. Bogo was not there, and there was no sign of Indrani. The neighbours huddled behind closed windows. After two hollers and a mild obscenity I went out of the yard. It was then I met Ramlal.

"Charlo, it is you boy?" he greeted me. "Boy, plenty take place since you gone," he spoke excitedly, as he nearly ran into me.

"Well, ah could see that because I don't see Bogo home, house lock up tight, tight, tight and the neighbours and them, the same thing but they peeping out only and not saying anything."

"Well, boy, them have a right, because Bogo gone on the rampage."

"How you mean?"

"You didn't hear wha' happen? Boy, is a long story since you leave. You remember after the fight, after Bogo beat Scottie and Victory, well, Sonnyboy couldn't take it and his own father was shamed because he say a penman take away his daughter-in-law and that his own son was useless. Well, Sonnyboy and the old man had a big quarrel. Sonnyboy never thought Bogo could beat them two champion stickman. So you know what happen next? They find Indrani behind the bamboo one night. She throat cut."

"When that happen?" I asked.

"Last week."

"Who do it?"

"Is Sonnyboy, everybody saying so because they find he hat in the same bush and the Land Rover tyre mark in the trace."

"And where Bogo?"

"Bogo gone mad same time boy, and went up the hill. He find Sonnyboy by No. 2 scale and beat him with that same stick until the man dead. Wasn't nice to see, boy, because he push the stick straight through the man mouth and leave it. Then he went by the pen afterwards, somebody say they see him leaving for the hills."

"When that was?"

"That was two days ago, Charlo."

Over the mule pens I looked towards the Bastahall hills, stark and grim against a watery sky. I hastened towards the cart standing near the water trough and soon, after a crack with my whip, the animal turned and bounded towards the track leading up to the winding incline. I stood on the cart, holding the reins.

About three miles up the tortuous climb the cart slowed down to a trot, then finally stopped. There the road narrowed and the sugar cane hemmed us in from both sides.

Gazing up to the undulating foothills, I looked for the ominous sign which soon came; a tiny speck, as motionless as a stone. I had to look for a second speck and when I found it, the third and fourth appeared not long afterwards with the same effortless turn in the air, round and round in a circle. The fifth and sixth hovering over a darker mass below confirmed the omen of death, and it was then that I knew I had found him.

The Girl from Bastahall

She lived in Bastahall, on a high, sunny ridge overlooking a pond and a grimy smoke stack of the sugar estate. He came from Bronte, fifteen miles south – a sunbaked village on white clay, surrounded by rolling canelands.

He saw her at Ramleela in the village market place and when their eyes met, he knew it was going to be she. But his parents did not like her manner and the way she spoke in that country-folk tongue. But to him, her eyes were fire and her touch was as gentle as her whispers, like the soft feathery arrow, atop the flowering sugarcane.

He met her again in the country and kissed her. And when they embraced, he felt her warm breasts next to his throbbing heart, breasts which would nurse the offspring that would be born unto them. He used to travel by train to visit her. She stood in the shadows on the railway platform beneath the projecting awning near the huge cistern, waiting. Her eyes lifted when the last wooden carriage rolled by, for she knew he always sat on those benches over the nutshell-littered floors, next to the brake van with the smoking wheels.

The poui trees were flowering in gold on the hills and the pomerac too, in its crimson blossoms, when he brought her home to his mother. Avoiding the bumps and ruts along the road, they laughed their way, riding between the canefields. When they coasted around the winding incline, he felt her shudder, hunching her shoulders until her long black hair lifted with the wind, and he smelt the fragrance of saffron and geera.

His mother disapproved of her as a daughter-in-law. So too, the father, but in his silence, he looked through the open window into fields of corn and cabbage and peas, knowing that in the harvest he would miss him. The time had come for him to leave, the time had come for him to dispel the fears and rumours that he wanted to play man in the house.

Pointing to the East with his crookstick, his ageing father demarcated the fertile plots and the shimmering fields in the rice lagoon they had sown together. All would be left for him, only if he would take as his wife, the dimpled, fair-skinned girl of the same district, daughter of Rajah, prosperous merchant and cane farmer.

But destiny ruled and in her hands passion claimed its course, stronger and more immutable than the mountains beyond, and deeper than the streams surrounding them. He chose the girl from Bastahall.

Their home was as he had imagined it to be – an ajoupa of four dirt walls, covered with carat which they had tied together over a mangrove framework. Their furniture was two wooden boxes, a cocoyea broom, and a hammock made out of crocus bags.

They slept on the bare ground, the smell of the good earth emanating through the jute sacks on which they lay. The cold walls of the mud hut bearing down upon them in that dank mustiness of wet grass and dry dung paste.

They found comfort in the bareness of the house, and even though they never spoke of love, their glances were full of it like the promises which were never made, but which were found in the loyalty that knitted their hearts.

Love blossomed bright like the sun overhead that shone on them as they worked together in the fields. Then a child was born, cementing the love of the parents. In the child, they saw their own likenesses and they marvelled at their own features. This increased their love for each other. They put the black ticka mark on its forehead and around its wrist; the black beads to ward off any 'maljo' evil.

The child cooed and bubbled with joy, changing hands from mother to doting father who now spent a great deal of time with his first born. Thrilled by his new found love, his devotedness to its mother was divided. But the mother's love remained unchanged, for she loved her husband and child with equal passion.

By the third year, he had saved enough money to buy the plots around his house, and the planting started with corn and peppers and melongene. With care and hard work, the crops blossomed. He bought a cow and a mule to take his produce to the market. He planted more and reaped in abundance. And all this time, the wife stood in the slush, knee deep, without pause or complaint, not knowing which day was Sunday. He remembered Rajah, the wealthy money lender of Carolina who now sat on his porch, rich and resigned from work.

Then one day, someone told him that his father had died and he was called home. In the little room where he had grown as a child, he saw his father in the open casket. The mother was weeping uncontrollably. His heart sank and now he felt some measure of remorse.

One day he saw Rajah's daughter, the one whom his mother wanted as his wife.

Something stirred inside him as he glanced at her, sitting poised and graceful, and he wondered what his life would have been, if he had married her instead. He thought of his own wife who now began to look so pale and haggard under the strain of work.

In Rajah's daughter he saw a new vitality, the same youthful spring in her bouncing steps, which his wife had at one time. He spent a week with his mother, comforting her in her sorrow. During this time, he became closer to the woman of whom his mother was so fond.

He walked the road confused, thinking of the woman with the slow, beguiling smile, and the long eyelashes. Her face appeared before him on his journey home and he could never forget. She held his arms; she yielded to him.

When he returned home, he was a changed man. He started to bicker and he quarrelled. He ignored his work in the garden; the animals starved, the crops wilted. Then he turned to drink. In his drunkenness he pulled his wife across the floor, knocking her down with his fists. This became the pattern of life.

Coming home late at nights drunk, he cursed and spat, ranted and rolled on the floor, as though some devil had seized him. The wife, now swollen from the continuous beating, remained patient and pleaded with him. But dutifully, she would still bring his tarrier of food with cuchilla and the red congo pepper and the lothar of rain water before him.

In the months that followed, the wife suffered more, and whatever little love there was left in her for him, it was destroyed when she learnt of his liaison with Rajah's daughter. She pined away, wrapped in her sorrow, seeking refuge in the care of her child who understood nothing.

One day it rained heavily, and finding her child asleep, she went into the lean-to shed at the back of the house. The bottle was on the shelf, dusty and half full. The red and black labels were discoloured with a brown stain. Hestitatingly, she reached out her hand, and an anguished gasp escaped her throat. She walked slowly back into the house. She looked at the garden that stretched out below her, where she had worked with her husband. When she closed the door behind her, a hush fell over the house, a silence almost as palpable as the liquid that had seeped down her throat. And for a long time after, only the loose carat stirred when a slight wind blew across the yard.

He came home late that afternoon swaggering, reeking of alcohol. Calling out loudly, he approached the door of the house. It was open. There was no sign of his child. When his eyes became accustomed to the dim interior, the sudden impact of death struck him with great force. For a moment he stood motionless. Then he bent over the still figures of his wife and his child, and a weariness came about his face, a sadness he could not explain. A small cry escaped his trembling lips, his nostrils twitched and his body shook.

Now he saw her in her quaint, awkward gait down the country road where he first met her, and there, hidden behind the railway cistern, where she waited for him. He remembered the glow of her cheeks when he took her home on his cycle. He recalled too, their tapia home, which they built together, their garden which they planted and reaped. The birth of their child out of the passion and love that grew between them, the long hours together in the fields and his little child who ran up his knees whenever he came home.

His stomach felt empty and his strength seemed to drain from his whole body. He stretched his hand over the black mass of hair that covered the child's face. He parted the skeins of hair, gently touching the fair cheeks he used to smother with his kisses. He moved slowly across to the body of his wife. There was froth on her mouth, staining the orhni covering one side of her face. There was the trickling stain of blood over her neck, running along her chest. But it could not hide the bruises, weals and blue welts that blotched her skin where he had pummelled her with his fists. Deliberating for a few more minutes, he placed his hand on her head. He then placed the corpses side by side. He stood up slowly and looked at them. His eyes moistened and the drops fell at his feet over them.

And when at long last, he tossed back his head as he was accustomed to do at Wong's and poured the remaining contents of the bottle into his mouth, the sun had long set, and lengthening shadows had already enveloped the small house. It was the first time in all those years that a light was not seen through the kitchen window in the early hours of the next morning, long before dawn.

Lalloo's Wrath

When Lalloo returned home from the garden in that vexatious mood, his trousers rolled up to his knees, he did not know that Dulcie had packed her bag and was long gone. She had left behind on the bed the crumpled heap of unstarched clothes, the empty phial of cheap khus-khus perfume and the two toothless combs with which she used to scratch her back after her baths in the rickety enclosure in the yard. With her hair long and straight like horsetail because she habitually anointed it with coconut oil, she used to stoop at the doorway combing it, showing off the mass of hair that dropped to her waist, taking so much pride in tossing it from side to side. Even as a child, walking to school, barefooted on the hot asphalt, the red *Westindian Readers* trussed under her arm, holding her little brother's hand, edging him to the side of the road, she showed that special care for her hair, having it bundled at the back of her head and never even wanting her mother to come near it.

Yesterday, Lalloo had struck her trembling cheeks, drawing blood, over an argument about food. Cold food she had served him, sitting cross-legged in the crocus bag hammock. His eyes blinked unsteadily from his bouts of rum drinking at Allong's shop, high up in the village. He joined hands and sang with his friends every payday over bottles of rum the shopkeeper replenished. Not until nine p.m., when the cane carts had long gathered at the estate cane-scale and the mules had been taken to the pens, would the shopkeeper push Lalloo through the heavy doors of the rum shop, while Lalloo tried still to convince everyone that he was able to walk straight.

Dulcie accepted the beatings from Lalloo as routine. After all, was he not her husband? Was it not his privilege to do just that, as one who had always provided for the house, as the man in the house, its master? Yet it had gone too far yesterday. He had grabbed hold of her hair, striking her again and again on her cheeks.

Lalloo entered the bedroom and saw the disarray of clothing and knew she had gone again.

He stood in the doorway, the loose carat over his head stirring in the slight breeze. The smell of cattle urine stifled him. A cloudiness seemed to aggravate his drowsiness which seized his whole body as he stood in a drunken stupor. Before him, before his squinting eyes, the sun blazed down over the flowering cane arrows that shimmered in the heat, like a coastal mirage of feathery white cane tops, like frothing waves over a green ocean. Only the road brought him to reality; the road, brown and dry, caked with ruts, stretched between the fields and the shaky wooden bridge over to Indian Trail, another village clinging onto a cliff near undulating canelands. There Dulcie's mother lived. And it was there Dulcie had gone.

He passed the chain through the hole in the door and doddered over the small patches of asphalt that covered the walk, in his hanging shirt-tails.He looked up the road, the four miles of blistering journey that would grill the soles of his canvas shoes. The journey was always painful. It was up this road, each time he quarrelled, each time he struck her with his clenched fists, slapped her with his stinging hands, that she would gather her skirt behind her and dash out of the house, returning later when he was sprawled drunk on the floor. She would take her meagre belongings, dress and orhini, and, holding the pair of rubber slippers in her hands, would run out into the road that would take her to her mother's home.

Outside, the rolling landscape was peaceful, but this did not relieve him of his solitude, out of which grew the alarming visions of disorder: the stack of unwashed wares, the unkempt rooms with the scattered clothing, the unswept yard. Other visions of Dulcie now increased his distress. He saw her lithe and brisk, hair wrapped, the fine sprinkling of sweat around her nostrils, small feet oiled, as she pattered about through narrow doorways, performing her household chores. He saw her wielding her cocoyea broom, one hand behind her back, the other in a continuous arch of movements over the mounds of gathering leaves and branches, which she would burn in the yard. But it was on afternoons that her hands were gentler, massaging his back as he stretched on his stomach on the empty rice bags over the earthen floor. She rubbed his shoulders with oil, sopping his head with vinegar and rum for the fever that would clutch his trembling body after working in the rain. He straightened himself. The drunkenness that had seized him in his calamity now drained out of him.

Now he stood before Dulcie's mother's home. The journey had sapped his strength, wetted his back, cleaned his head of the dizziness. He looked up at the little porch where the bottles of achar and hot sauce were fermenting in the sun, feeling somewhat small as he called out to her in a voice that was not his own.

The house stood on shaky stilts, mouldering shingles, as if leaning on the front steps, which themselves seemed in need of support. There was a wooden bench downstairs and an axe that stood against it with garden tools. Behind the house of raw unpainted boards under the sepia, rusting galvanized sheets, the sky was a cerulean backdrop, its brightness blotched by a solitary corbeau hovering, circling lazily. Lalloo squinted at the bird as he imagined himself aloft, floating on the breezy cloud embankments, gazing down at the parched burnt-siewna plots where he worked, spent most of his own life. He saw the same fields which he ploughed, the land, in varying, faded tones divided by drains, some a glassy glint on the surface of stagnant water. Further to the right, past his own ajoupa, the land receded, dissolving in colour and shape in the background where the mangrove ran like green dykes separating sea from land and the glitter of the settling ooze blurred in the shallows in the distance.

He called again.

Dulcie appeared, the same tender figure, shaken from his onslaught. The sadness was still stamped on her face.

"What you want now?" she asked, a little more weight in her voice as she stood in her mother's gallery.

"Dulcie, ah come for you."

"Come for me, after all that licks?"

"Doh mind dat, gul. You know how I does get on, sometimes," he pleaded.

"Is rum talking still?"

He was peeved, his confidence shattered, standing like a child in its plea for candy, the width of his shoulders narrowed. He realised that the frustrating loneliness would increase by her refusal to accompany him home.

"Not coming back – not going, and I done make up my mind." The words descended on his head like thunder, its peals bursting in his brain. The dizziness came back, the sickening feeling; he felt cold even in the sun.

"Gawd." He answered feebly and the realisation came to him, like a clout behind his head, causing him to press forward, stumbling on wobbly legs as in the past when his mother drove him out of the yard, a little boy going to school. He advanced.

"Gul, you serious? Come leh we goh home nah. I won't do it again." He spoke in a pleading voice.

"Ah not coming! Everytime is the same ting and you goh beat me again."

"Ah tell you, it goh be awright. Last chance, now."

"No! Ma done tell me dat we finish. I make up me mind this time."

High over the house, the corbeau circled slowly in the same slow turns, a dot in the sky. He felt as lonely as the bird.

Again the sense of loss gripped him as his eyes descended from the sunlit skies on to the house top and then on to Dulcie, still standing in the shadows, leaning over the banister rail. She remained quiet, pensive, orhini wrapped around her cheeks, covering her mouth in disdain, looking down on him in the yard, a broken figure; he, rapt and tortured, looked into her eyes for an answer that would appease the pang of despair. Lalloo felt his feet sinking on the hot sand. He kept staring into Dulcie's face. She looked away, the beating he had given her was still in her mind; she remembered his rage, his strong hands that shook her, raised her off her feet, dashing her against the wall. She felt the pain around her stomach and on her bruised thighs where he had kicked her. Her neck was still blue where he had collared her. Tears.

Now Lalloo stood below her, disappointed that she decided to remain at her mother's home. He recoiled from her decision which increased his anguish. He sweated, his eyes smarted. He did not remember her answering him like that before. He felt weak, tired; suddenly aged, becoming useless. So she had made up her mind. He saw himself like the corbeau over the house top, away from the other birds, circling foolishly, desperately, its waning senses too feeble for survival. Suddenly a new fever seized him as he trembled in the sand. He roared: "You not coming back eh? Answer me!"

The old ferocity had returned, firing his eyes, detonating in his voice that was calm only a moment ago.

Dulcie turned sharply towards him. His hands were at his waist, the sun blinding him. She did not see them but she imagined the terror in them. She had known their power before. At the tone of his voice she jumped. Lalloo came forward slowly. She grasped her orhini and retreated. He approached the house, coming out of the sun. She watched; he kept on walking.

"You not coming eh, eh? Not coming you say?" he ranted.

He had passed the steps, his eyes staring past her into space. He ripped his shirt off his back and tore at his vest. He kept on walking, muttering to himself, dazed as though lost in another world, until he disappeared under the house. She was puzzled. She cautiously looked down from the banister to catch a glimpse of him. After a little while she heard noises, thumping, chopping sounds. She came down the steps slowly and felt the whole house tremble. The house shook; then she felt the floor tilt, heard cracking noises. She ran further down the steps. Lalloo had seized the axe and, like a demon, was savagely swinging it against the stilts.

With his head bent low, he swung the axe in wide arcs, the blade striking the centre post. Destruction. Again and again on to the same spot. Dulcie felt another crumbling noise, breaking joists. The floor snapped. The walls leant, sank. Eyes bulging in fright, she ran down the last treaders into the yard. Part of the house crashed behind her. The rumbling noise was deafening. Between the strokes, she heard his mumbling, interrogative voice, "Not coming back, eh?", repeated in the din.

He was attacking the last stilt with the same savage fury of a madman, the crumbling, decaying boards collapsing in a heap over him, the dust rising in clouds. She rushed out of the yard at top speed, this time down the road from which she had come the night before. She did not look back.

Afterwards, there was silence over the shattered remnants of the fallen house. The dust settled over it and sailing high above, only the corbeau hovered in its continuing, dreamy, circular movements, a solitary speck in the quiet afternoon sky.

Curse of Mazay

When Hossam was alive that night, sneering at us, his cheeks etched by bloodless furrows of flesh and his shoulders draped with that decaying shroud that looked so gruesome no one at the card table looked at him as he stood in the shadows leaning against the door. Only once, Sada, sitting like some castrated bull with his grizzly shock of beard, gazed into his bloodshot eyes.

Hossam had just returned home from smoothing the mound of earth over his brother, earth cold as the starless night that seemed to further smother the dead. In the room the tongue of flame atop the flambeau ascended like a gold tipped spear, aspiring to sooty smoke overhead, casting shadows on stucco walls. Malo threw a queen of diamonds on the table and the flame flickered. Otherwise, a gloomy silence pervaded the chamber, four men crowded over cards from which colour had long fled. Through the crevices of the only window came the night's noises, but the rotted boards seemed to bar us from the eerie wail of winds careening off the forest walls.

Then suddenly we heard those screams piercing the stillness and Hossam was no longer standing behind us. Somehow, we sensed something in the room, some invisible object that moved about causing the air to stir around us and Hossam was at once seen to clutch at his throat, struggling as though with some unseen force that tossed him from corner to wall. The door banged with the wind that rushed inside in a howl; Malo shielded the flame, the hat rack rattled on its hook and the brass lamp over us swung like a pendulum, creaking at the chain from the ceiling. Horridly loud, the screams had come from those secret, abysmal regions of distant marshlands smothered in perpetual twilight. We turned our heads. On the floor were traces of mud. Streaks of dirt were on the door on which Hossam had leant. Malo got up and touched the brown stains.

"From Timital," he muttered. Timital was the village cemetery, five miles away, beyond the swamp lands, where in the dismal solitude a lonely gull would stand guard on some dead stump surrounded by the buzz of marshland flies.

"Christ, from Timital?" Sada asked himself, face drawn like shredded cloth and his matted brows a tangle of forest weeds. "And in the middle of the night," he added...

We huddled together as the flame now danced on the table. Sada stretched and pulled the door shut. The bolt was driven home. We felt a sense of relief and security. Hossam had seemed to just disappear through that door. The trace of mud on the door posts and on the floor bore evidence of his struggle with some supernatural demon that spirited him away, right under our noses.

We waited in silence, our breathing distinctly audible in the quietness of the room when, in some unaccountable and inexplicable way, we now sensed something lurking outside the house, whose presence was somewhat bewildering and mysterious. We had long abandoned our cards on the table. The faces of kings and queens bordered with embroidered regalism stared up at us with sublime vanity. Sada tugged at his coat and pressed forward, his thick beard almost brushing his knees; Carlo, rooted in dreaded anguish, shuddered in anticipation of another frantic scream. Malo cowered beneath the ghostly light of the flambeau, his eyes glued to the door through which the invisible power of Evil would penetrate at any time. I was calm but I could not restrain the palpitations of my heart which raced uncontrollably. Malo sweated at the forehead; Sada's eyes bulged white; Carlo shivered. And the apprehension of Evil gripped us in silence when the wind subsided. Fidgety and restless now, Carlo kept staring at the door, shifted around us and broke our watchful spell. Malo turned on his chair and we stood up.

"Looks like we have to find Hossam," Sada whispered, the rasping tone of his throat seemingly quietened by the fear that held us together.

"Right. But how we going outside in that blackness? And it cold like hell!"

So we got up, closed the door behind us. Malo led the way, flambeau in hand, the flame jumping with every breath of wind, throwing our grosteque shadows on the walls of the house. Malo grasped his truncheon; Sada, his long staff. I held my cutlass. The path led down the incline over loose gravel and dead leaves, gathered in heaps at the wide entrance, narrowing to a track that unravelled itself between high grass on the river embankment. We peered behind thickets that seemed to spring up at every turn, hulking masses in the shadows behind which the presence of Evil loomed in every quiver of branch, each snap of twig or crackle of dead leaves under our feet. The river leadened beneath the glow of a rising moon that cast spectral light over the mountain range. With their roots immersed in slush, stringy water weeds curtained off the span downstream beyond which the lake broadened into an expanse of mud and ooze. We trudged steadily, the cold night brooding over our shoulders, the solitary feeble flame like a guiding light, held in Malo's hand before him as he led us across the terrain to that small plot in search of Hossam.

It was only when we reached the middle of the marshland swamp bordering the elevated cemetery plots that Malo spoke about Mazay.

"You know, that man vowed revenge. How he felt he was wronged."

"Don't make jokes," I said, lopping off the shrubs before me.

"I am telling you, before he died, he stayed eight months in the hospital."

"What he was sick with?"

"That terrible thing that covers your whole skin with sores and bumps."

"You mean, he was a leper?"

"Leprosy," Sada echoed as he leant on his staff.

"Christ, that disease eats you piece by piece."

"Had no cure for him, poor fellow," Malo said.

"Well, that was not the worst part. You know, Shairoon was the real cause for him to suffer in all that bitterness."

"What you mean?" Malo asked.

"She went to live with Hossam, you know, I don't know if you could blame her but Hossam used to go with her to the hospital to see him, and they got friendly. What you could do about that?" Sada said.

"Christ, he grieved like hell. He vowed he was coming back for Hossam." Malo shook his truncheon.

Twice we stumbled over mossy logs criss-crossing the path that led to banks of thorns and blacksage, and rising from the soggy earth where we fell, the soft mud still on the palms of our hands, we came right up to Timital. The lake stretched before us on the left.

"Where to turn now?" Malo asked.

"Look, keep right," Sada said pointing with his staff.

"Christ, I could scarcely see me own foot!"

The flambeau bobbed before us as Malo tripped and stumbled. We held him up, pulling at his hairy coat.

Further on, amongst the crude timber crosses strapped with vines, and the stakes that were driven lopsided over elevated mounds, we strayed between mossy headstones, the carved letterings eroded by time. Sada lumbered before me, Malo lifted the flambeau in search of the new grave under which Mazay lay. Tall trees, immortelles, stood over us. Vines tangled, hung like a huge net blocking the moon.

We stood among the graves in the moonlight, invading the privacy of the dead, the bleak river wind cold on our cheeks. Frogs chanted their weird chorus of croaks under wavering fireflies. Then we heard the spine-chilling shrieks again. We jumped, grasping at one another, Sada's coarse coat rubbing on my arms.

Before us, beneath the row of immortelles, something moved, something which had been waiting for us behind the hanging vines and cluster of branches. The swamp smelt of herbs and a perfumed mist seemed to rise out of the ground, stifling us with a nauseating scent that came from the flowers along the river banks. But our eyes were stuck to the undergrowth beneath the immortelles in the little grove. We did not advance any further, for the noises continued, coming from the contorted, writhing shapes before us. Noises that were neither human nor animal, but nevertheless terrifying in their phantasmal agony. We stood rooted in the deep slush amongst the tombstones, struck at the horror of demons, struggling, twisting between the network of vines and branches. The shapes moved deeper into the woods. Further away. We gathered courage and followed. The groaning noises seemed to beckon us as if by some supernatural calling, luring us by a magical spell.

We entered the grove, the low branches of the trees touched our heads. The object that hung ten meters away before us appeared shapeless and black. We came close to it, Malo raised the flambeau; it was Hossam's shroud. Sada pushed it off with his long staff. Then we heard those blood-tingling shrieks again inside the grove. We halted. The flambeau in Malo's hand shook. Two panting, thrashing forms seemed to be locked now in a fierce struggle, one dragging the other over the forest floor while the night winds howled around us. We were never able to get close enough to them because they went deeper and deeper into the woods groaning and hissing and convulsing in pain, until the spectral apparitions disappeared.

They found us the next day five miles from Timital, steeped in mud, away from the swampland, wandering and spent; Sada, dazed, jabbering incoherently, the flambeau still in Malo's hand, but cold and unlighted. They said, in a twitter of laughter, that my cutlass was trussed into my waist band, my mouth was full of weeds and I looked like a madman.

As for Hossam, we were never able to find out what really became of him, swallowed in the mire of the Timital burial ground, hauntingly peaceful and desolate where the one gull, like some monopode, always stood on the dried stump over the swamp guarding the dead, and where under slush between mossy headstones he had buried his brother only the night before.

No Pork, Cheese

It was in the middle of croptime in Bastahall. The heat came from a hot sky and erupted out of the ground in shimmering waves, grilling the blades of grass. It rose into the skirts of the cane cutters. Hog-cattle groaned under heavy loads, their mouths dripped, their heavy rumps reddened sore from the prodding sticks.

Ahamad, the muleman, tied his mount to one of the four outer posts of the village rum shop. He pushed his soiled hat to the back of his head, squinted and came into the bar.

"Petit quart, Wong," he pounded the counter with his fists. "Not that watery mixture from below the counter, eh?"

"Hush, choopit, you foolish or what?" Wong glared from behind his thick lenses.

"Dat cacapool does gimme real headache; seventy overproof or nothing," Ahamad reminded him.

"You all time talking chit," Wong bellowed.

"Ah doh know if is chit, but you giving me plenty chat now," Ahamad roared.

"Amat, sot you dam mow eh," Wong shouted.

Ahamad sprinkled a few drops of rum on the ground around his feet. With one hand he held his hat against the back of his head and in a loud gulp, downed his drink. He wiped his mouth with the back of his other hand, coughed, placed the empty glass on the counter and spat freely on the floor.

"Ah, Wong, dat one strong, boy. Like you take it straight from the cask."

Two men came into the shop and sat near Ahamad. One was Balraj, the other Bhola. Both had the same black, scrubby features; black hands, blacker at their chests and around their necks where the cane-ash smudged into layers of grime and sweat.

"Gimme two more glasses, Wong," ordered Ahamad.

Wong wiped the wet counter with a dirty rag and brought two upturned glasses. Ahamad sniffed at the counter.

"Lord, Wong, you bring dat nasty salt kine cloth again and stink up the place!" Ahamad complained.

"He is Muslim, Wong. You know what dat mean?" Balraj said.

"Salt kine good meat, Amat," Wong smiled.   "Dat good for creoni," Ahamad grumbled.

Bhola laughed, turned to Wong over the counter and asked: "Dem glass clean, Wong?"

"No smelly lime in it?" Wong asked.

"Bring a flask ah Cockspur and mark it," Ahamad ordered.

Wong got out of his alpagatas, climbed on the rice barrel, stretched his hand and took down a bottle of rum. While Ahamad broke the seal from the bottle, the other two men rinsed their glasses.

"You know dat rum eh have no kinda taste again?" Bhola asked.

"Which one?"

"White star."

"How you mean? All dem old brand like Black Label, Forres Park and Mount Gay gone out ah style. Dese days is strictly Eclipse and how you call dat brand again?" Balraj asked.

"Vat?"

"No. Sugar cane brandy! Look it dey."

"Yes, dat well cure and I have to give puncheon a rest. What! Dat TDL is something else. Like dat rum ent have time to cure, boy."

They sat on their stools with their elbows on the counter and gazed at the shelves of liquor. Rows and rows of bottles with discoloured labels stood in a quiet line.

They poured the rum with unhurried movements, measuring the height of the drinks against one another's glass. Then, with that quick deliberate curve of their arms, with glasses to their lips, they drank in unison. They smacked their lips, twisted their faces, spat, and wiped their mouths with the back of their hands. By 1.00 p.m. they had consumed two bottles of Cockspur.

They rocked on their stools and splashed their drinks all over the counter. Their eyes took on a mischievous glaze, like wet rock salt.

Ahamad was generous in pouring, but his hand shook and soon his drink of red rum spilled. Wong ran up hurriedly with his rag, but the rum had leaked between the counter boards onto bags of peas.

Balraj rose from his stool, took Wong's rag and continued wiping the counter. But Wong was outraged. His eyes bulged larger than his lenses.   "Dammit! You drunk or what? You goh pay for it," Wong threatened.

"Mark it down man, Wong. Is not the whole bag you goh charge me for."

After the third bottle emptied and the level of the fourth passed the middle of the label, Balraj got up. He announced that he was going to make a pump and wobbled away to the urinal.

The other two said they wanted to have their 'pumps' too. It was evident from the relief on Ahamad's face when he returned that he had made good use of his twenty minutes in the urinal.

It was Balraj's turn to order now.

"Bottle a Cockspur again, Wong. Mark it in my name. Will fix you up payday Friday."

Wong looked over his shopscale, where he was attending to a customer.

"Jink enof alledy."

"Doh fraid man, Wong."

"Ah cutting cane man – mark it. Ah getting paid Friday."

Wong brought a bottle of Cockspur for them, scribbled on a pad of brown paper, then hurried back to the other customer at the counter. Balraj held the bottle, poured and once more missed the glasses. Bhola got up from his stool, groped towards the door and held on to the post. Outside the glare was strong; the dried cane trash collected in stringy bundles. In his attempt to hawk and spit clear across the width of the road, Bhola lost his balance and stumbled forward. Ahamad doddered to his rescue, grabbed Bhola by the belt and collar and dragged him inside.

"Christ, like you charge up ahready?" Balraj asked as he dribbled.

"Ah tell you Cockspur doh agree wid me at all!" Bhola blurted.

After his third trip to the urinal, Ahamad returned holding up his unbuttoned pants. He swaggered towards the bar and stepped into the spittoon.

"Christ, you mean ah drunk ahready, boy."

"Look you goh drown. Right in dat mess," Bhola said.

"You know what happen? Ah feeling hungry now. Wong, what you have dey? Bring some cheese ... cut up with pepper!"

Bhola poured again and asked for more ice. Balraj started to sing. The cheese came in a yellow saucer with three matchsticks sticking out of it.

"Wong, hope you eh find dem matchsticks on the floor," Ahamad joked.

"Ground clean, clean, man. Wash it every month," Wong replied quickly.

Ahamad mistakenly took up Balraj's glass and Balraj coughed into Bhola's face. Ahamad braced himself over the counter and with thumb and index finger seized a slice of cheese, lifting it up over his mouth. He closed one eye and the cheese hovered over his face. He lurched forward and betted that the cheese would fall right into his mouth; Balraj took up the challenge. Bhola shouted,"Move to the left." The cheese descended from Ahamad's unsteady hands and fell into his open eye.

"Lord, pepper in me... "

"Eye," Bhola prompted him.

"Watch you language. People buying in the shop," Balraj reminded him.

Ahamad bawled out. He coughed and cursed. He moved around in a circle as though in a game of blind man's bluff. He rubbed his eyes with the dirty shirtsleeve until cane-ash was smeared all over his tear-filled face.

"Water!" he roared, his face a black mess.

Balraj drifted to the counter and brought the water bottle, while Bhola turned to steady Ahamad in a standing position. Balraj held the water over Ahamad's head.

"Doh keep me waiting as if you want to baptise me."

The hand with the water circled over his head then tilted. The water came down in a gush over his face and drenched him.

"Christ, the wrong eye again."

Two women, buying in the dry goods section of the shop, were amused at the commotion, seeing that the theatrical skit was performed by their own villagers.

It was now five thirty p.m. and the men began to sing and drum on the counter top. Balraj knocked the water bottle with a crown cork. Ahamad, recovering from the effect of pepper, sang in Hindi with his left eye closed, in a strange wavering falsetto. Bhola smacked his lips, imitating a drum. Balraj demanded another flask while Ahamad wanted bread and cheese. Bhola turned to Wong.

"Look, Wong, ah feel to eat some meat too – and ham. Bring two ounces."

"No ham, only loce pok."

"Right," Bhola said. "Mark it. Better bring half pound. And slice it up."

With a long knife, Wong cut six loaves of hops with the bits of dried leaves still clinging to the bottom of the bread. He inserted his pork and cheese filling and shook the pepper sauce bottle expertly over the sandwiches. He quickly deposited the waiter before the three drinkers and walked over to the customers who were rapping on the counter.

They sang loudly, all three joined in the chorus. Their hair was dishevelled, their shirts were out of their trousers and Ahamad's wet sleeves were unrolled, flapping on the counter. His face took on a dazed look, his lower jaw dropped and his eyes rolled like agates.

They continued drinking, with relaxed regularity, between mouthfuls of roast pork. They sang *O Danny Boy,*

ending up with the last verse of *Clementine*. Suddenly
Ahamad stopped in the middle of the last stanza. With his
mouth wide open, he held onto his stomach. He turned to
the others, his eyes rolled. "Christ! Is poke all you gimmie."

Balraj choked on his drink, spattering rum and Bhola
raised both arms to shield off the spray. With terror in his
bulbous eyes, Ahamad pushed Bhola and Balraj aside and
wobbled out of the shop through the side door into the
road.   He tried to balance himself, then drifted towards
the drain near the urinal. There, stooping over the running
water, he coughed and groaned. His eyes reddened in the
ordeal and his nose dripped. He pushed his fingers into his
throat in an attempt to regurgitate all that he had eaten.
Balraj stood at the rumshop door, shaking with laughter and
Bhola, looking on, could only say, "Wong, no poke, man.
Cheese de man want."

The people in the shop came outside and Wong stood
behind his glasses, mouth agape, while Ahamad belched
and ranted. He rolled on the ground and his whole face was
smeared with sand. He looked like a clown.

Darkness descended. Wong closed his shop doors.

Overcome with Cockspur, Balraj and Bhola were left
outside under the shed. They sat quietly, heads turning from
side to side. The spittle drooped from their mouths in long
streaks like wet gossamer threads. Now and then a groan
escaped their mouths. But with Ahamad it was continuous –
the coughing and bellowing noises – as he squatted, stradled
over the drain, with his fingers deep in his throat.

Only the mule remained silent in the darkness, its head
bowed, still tethered to the shop post where Ahamad had
left it at ten-thirty that morning.

Assam's Iron Chest

A dull moon glowed in the country-night darkness. They came out of hiding from behind the caimette tree, avoiding the crackle of dead leaves underfoot. Into the pale light stepped big, loudmouthed Mathias, Boyo, with his matted dreadlocks wrapped up in a 'Marvingay' hat, and laglee-chewing Sagamouth, so nicknamed because of his grotesque lips and the smattering noises they made.

In the little clearing overlooking Assam's shopyard, they waited patiently behind large tannia leaves that shielded them from the light of passing motorists. They waited for the last bus to rattle by on its return journey to town and for the soft glow of Assam's Coleman lamp, whirring moths and beetles striking against the lampshade, to go out.

Boyo puffed at the carmine-tipped stick of ganja that brightened his face as he slapped at mosquitoes. Sagamouth's lips continued slurping noisily.

"Keep quiet, man. Christ! You goh wake up the whole damn village," Mathias hissed between clenched teeth.

"Look, the light out," Sagamouth whispered excitedly.

"Yea, but keep your flapping mouth shut. I could see. Who in charge here?"

"Boyo, put out that weed. Whole place stink ah grass," Mathias warned.

At the galvanised paling surrounding the shop-yard, a flimsy steel sheet suddenly loosened in the moonlight and fell aside, allowing three figures to squeeze through the narrow space into the shop-yard. They were confronted by stacks of empty soft drink crates, discarded cartons, pitch oil tins and, against the shed, bundles of stacked crocus bags.

Remembering the action in the motion picture *Bataan*, and with the dramatic invasion in *Desert Fox* still fresh in his mind, Mathias crouched on all fours, leading his platoon across the yard.

"Sssh," he cautioned them as he sat on his buttocks before the big door. They paused in the darkness. Mathias' hands felt for the door frame. He inserted a pig foot into the crevice. With both feet against the wall he pried the door, throwing his whole weight on it. A slow cracking noise erupted as the nails lifted off the hinges and the door came up. A dank odour of wet oilmeal, soap and stale mackerel greeted them. They crawled in, feeling their way between the stacks of packaged goods. Further inside, they saw a table with a lighted lamp and a red spot of mosquito coil under it. A big square mosquito net hung over a four-poster bed out of which floated Assam's snores in grating spasms.

Convinced that Assam was sound asleep, Mathias struck a match and immediatley shadows jumped across the walls, on the shelves of bottles and over tinned stuffs. On the floor, crowding the aisles, was the paraphernalia of jumbled haberdashery, pots and pans, and bags of peas and beans. Moving in the crowded interior, Mathias came to the room where, over a small table, bills hung pinned to the wall, next to a Chinese calendar. Cupping the lighted match in his hand, Mathias tiptoed further inside. More bags, packed in rows, and bales of macaroni and cornmeal. Flagons of cider and an old rum cask stood on the floor. In the corner, the square block of metal stood on a rough framework of local timber; a squat, dull hunk of iron with a circular dial of brass. It was the iron chest. Mathias came up to it and tested its weight. Boyo braced himself in readiness.

With Sagamouth holding the light, Mathias and Boyo heaved at the heavy hulk of iron. They pushed until the wooden stand inched along the floor.

"Damn thing must be full," Boyo said.

"Canefarmer pay, choopid," Sagamouth replied, spraying them with his spittle.

"All you keep quiet," Mathias entreated.

Pitting themselves against the heavy load, they worked with caution. Twice they heard Assam cough. Their hands glided, slipped over the smooth surface of the chest. After some strenuous efforts, they managed to push the chest to the doorway. Finally the whole bulk of metal was heaved outside, catapulting, digging into the yard with a dull thud.

The cool night breeze invigorated their bodies. The sight of the chest inspired their minds with the promise of new things in life. Sagamouth disappeared into the bushes and returned with a crocus bag containing a crowbar, a sledge hammer and a flambeau. Behind him he dragged a large piece of board, the underside of which was lined with plain galvanised sheeting. At one end was tied a long piece of rope. They eased their cargo on to the wooden contraption. Mathias again directed the operations. Standing before the metal chest, he tied the end of the rope around his waist and leant forward. Boyo and Sagamouth were pushing at the rear.

They hauled the makeshift sledge along the grassy side tracks. With the heavy iron chest strapped to it, it skidded and scuttled across the bare ground. Their backs shone like their faces, which streamed with perspiration. Boyo puffed like a trace mule. Sagamouth's mouth continued its feeble movements. They halted behind a silk cotton tree. Mathias swung the axe in long, measured strokes against the chest. The sounds echoed deep into the woods. The heavy blows ricocheted over the door. Now and then he stopped to inspect the shallow indentations. The brass handle had fallen off, the dial long warped under the punishing blows. Yet the door remained sealed. They persevered, taking turns with the sledge hammer and the crowbar, until Mathias, bringing the heavy hammer from high overhead, struck the chest with such force that they heard a loud cracking noise.

Instantly they sprang forward, their eager hands reached out for the door. Three pairs of hands churned inside the chest, as their eyes opened in anticipation. Then Sagamouth withdrew exclaiming, "Empty."

"Christ, you mean the damn thing en't have a cent, boy."

"All dis damn trouble," Boyo said.

Mathias stood up wearily and looked at the others, his arms sore and wet, as he whispered, "Dat damn Chinese smart like hell! Ah never cud believe it. You mean he move out all de damn money, boy?"

Sagamouth's dribbling stopped. Boyo looked up at the sky.

One day, some three months afterwards, when the notorious episode was almost forgotten in the little village and the blue police van had long completed its trips to

Assam's on investigation, Sagamouth came into Assam's shop. He stood at the counter and called for a pound of saltbeef. There was no one in the shop except for a well-dressed man. A briefcase was on the counter and he was busily scribbling on a pad.

"Yes, please sign on this, Mr Assam," the man said in his mellow voice. Assam, spectacles tied to his ear with a piece of flour-bag string, leant over the counter and scrawled on the pad.

"Have everything dong, Mister Blong?"

"Yes, all that you have told me," Mr Brown replied. "$1,000 in US, $15,000 in Canadian and $2,100 in TT cash. $89 in silver and that solid gold chain from China. But as I said, I'm not sure that the company will pay the foreign money."

Assam placed a large brown paper bag containing two bottles of rum on the counter before Mr Brown.

"Well, check all in TT dollars then," Assam said, taking out another brown bag from below the counter.

Mr Brown smiled and pointed to the last item on the list. "Ah – that is the iron chest, Mr Assam. The company will pay you the $8,000 you have claimed."

"Yes, sah," Assam said smiling, "velly goot," his eyes two narrow slits behind thick lenses.

Sagamouth stood dumb, rooted in front of the counter, unmoving, as he listened to the conversation. His lips had suddenly lost all sense of movement. They hung droopily over the counter, nearly falling into the shop-scale pan.

Moro

Moro arrived in Esperanza late one afternoon in an antiquated Chevrolet loaded with bamboo cages filled with game cocks. Like other cock breeders who moved from district to district in Trinidad, he was carefree and enjoyed a cavalier bachelorhood. Moro's leatherlike, spice-coloured cheeks jutted beneath eyes that shone with the mirth of songs. A single plait of rich, dark hair was held at the back of his head by a twist of crimson ribbon.

Moro sat as if welded to the seat, his short frame in stark contrast to the long arms that gripped the wheel.

"Hi-yahh!" he called pleasantly as the clanking car rolled to a halt.

Moro's Doms and Clarets had conquered the fiercest Reds and Greys from St. Raphael, Valencia and Malgrétoute. His birds were victorious in Rancho Quemado and even in La Brea where the cocks were almost night-black, like the pitch that oozed from the great lake around them.

Moro was serious in his training. He would stoop for hours with his legs parted, keeping his forearms laced up, protected from the spurs. He pushed the game cocks between and around his legs in a figure eight, taunting them until their heads reddened with rage and their beaks snapped open for battle. Again and again he tossed their lithe bodies aloft, their long clean necks toughened by continuous massage with bayrum and clove. With his hands beneath the long tails, he pushed them up and away, their wings flapping in the air, their beaks and spurs arched forward and moving at a devastating speed. Then he would put them on a rope stretched tautly between the paling and a tree in the yard. There they would rock back and forth until their leg muscles finally hardened under the strain and their talons tightened.

Moro followed the same routine each day, beginning before dawn with a quick shower and black coffee, his life as disciplined as that of the birds. Then he would gently bring out the game cocks, speaking quietly to them, blowing his warm breath on their heads, caressing the combs so their backs arched in response. They tipped their heads to listen to his whispers and the mellow monotone of his deep, soothing voice. Then, suddenly, the peaceful scene would be changed by the early morning breeze which scattered the dead leaves in the yard and ruffled the down on the birds. As their feathers lifted, the thick muscular thighs would be exposed and a fierceness would come into their eyes. It was the same sharp ferocity that appeared in the gayelle at the moment of battle.

Moro was working with his birds one morning when a long, blue Buick pulled into the yard. Through the bougainvillea Moro was able to see the white sidewall tyres and a glint of chrome, but he did not recognise the man who stepped from behind the wheel. He was black, middle-aged, and his face was crumpled and tired-looking. He wore a faded khaki shirt which was wet at the armpits.

"Morning."

Moro nodded, but did not move. The man moved towards him, with a limp in his heavy stride.

"You is Moro, the cockfighter?"

Moro turned towards the visitor, putting down a cock on a bamboo pole.

"What is it?"

"Boss send me. Want to see you...is about game cocks. What to tell him? He say you must come up."

Moro frowned. "Wey he living?"

"Never hear about Mr Holman? He is the overseer in Caroni. House by de side road after Milton Number Two. One ah dem backra quarters, white and green windows. Big yard."

"You mean the boss in the game? How much cocks he have?" Moro asked.

The black man shrugged. "Is plenty and all kind. You coming?"

Moro nodded.

The next day he stood before the white mansion, enthralled by its green tarpaulin awnings and fine mosquito netting in a paler shade. The estate was magnificent, the house stood on whitewashed concrete pillars surrounded by potted palms.

Moro heard the sudden crow of a cock. Then the chicken run came into view, running through the pillars at the back of the building.

"Mr Holman!" he called, trying to make himself heard over the crowing cocks penned in the coops. "Mr Holman! Mr Holman!" he yelled louder, his growing anxiety obvious in his voice.

A tall man, clad all in white, came down the back steps. He shook hands with Moro.

Moro felt the power of the big man.

"Hear about you, man," Mr Holman spoke in a

surprisingly soft voice. "Think you could fly my birds for me? Look after them? Will pay you well, man."

Holman did not wait for a reply, but turned to lead the way into the great house, passing the Buick with its cloth hood down, its fancy metallic buttons on the dashboard standing out in contrast to the soft leather upholstery. There were clothes hanging on a line strung between the huge pillars at the back of the house.

They descended the concrete aisle, the coops arranged wall to wall high off the ground so that the droppings would fall and be washed away by the continuous rush of water below. The cells were constructed of expanded wire mesh, each separated by solid polished pitch pine walls to prevent the birds from seeing one another. Inside, the cocks stood on two-inch diameter perches, swaying and crowing in a continuous staccato of piercing cries.

"That is Satan," Holman pointed. "Black Devil never lost a battle yet. Watch that beak and how he shakes his head from the right to the left...so fast. That is the sign of a good fighter. This one is Banana Bottom, champion of champions, a legend for destroying over twenty-five cocks and," Holman smiled, "bringing in $22,000 for me."

"Nice cocks, Mr Holman," Moro complimented. "They looking good, man."

"Not good enough, Moro."

"What you mean?"

"Ever heard of De Pas and Vasquez?"

Moro nodded.

"The greatest cocks are from Cuba...Vasquez. He is a fanatic," Holman explained. "You heard of him. Well, whenever there is a fight and he attends, the gayelle is closed until he is through."

"Why is that?"

"Man, he is crazy about fighting cocks. Have you heard of St. Eves and Guichard from Martinique, Malaban from Guadeloupe? Well, Little Guadeloupe is getting strong breeds from France and Puerto Rico, Hernandez and dos Pasos from Santo Domingo and de Jesus from Haiti. They are the giants in cock fighting...they are the giants from Guadeloupe and Martinique. These are crazy men, wild about cocks. They would leave their wives for their battlers, starve for them. They give them only the very best. Their coops are under mosquito netting to avoid sandflies. It is honey in the morning and boiled eggs and greens in the evening," Holman shook his head. "I tell you, Moro, they count every grain of cracked corn, every capsule of vitamins. They record their rest periods, hours of sleep... they even count the drops of water the birds drink. They know when their birds will sneeze, when they will cough, and in the ring they know exactly at what time the opponent's cock will strangle on its own blood and when it will be torn to shreds. They never lose, Moro. Never. They live cocks. They breed and breathe cocks. They are the champions, Moro. ...for now they are the champions. But you know something?"

Moro nodded. He did know.

"I have to beat them," Holman said, his eyes piercing Moro's with an intense stare. "I must win. Otherwise all my efforts will have been in vain. I have everything, Moro ...feed, medicines, nice pens, the best birds. Five of the cocks are from Cuba out of Vasquez's own broods. Only the trainer is missing, and I think that is you."

"Why me?"

"Because I have a challenge. Ever heard of El Diablo?"

Moro turned excitedly. "Yes, dat's the greatest cock in the Caribbean, man. Dat from Santo Domingo."

Holman rubbed his hands together anxiously. "Well, they have challenged us, but Motilal and Rienzi...you know Rienzi, the big man from the north...they both refused."

"They have a right to refuse. Boss, everybody know about dat game cock. It is the baddest thing with spurs," Moro said. "It kill Corriea bird and Clarke, two champions, one after the other. Man cry too bad when dey see dat bird. Money lost, lots a money lost, and Corriea hold he head and bawl because his cock was the greatest thing to pass through Valencia...bad as Banana Boat, he was."

The men stepped from the runs into the sunshine and walked to the low shed.

"So, what you think?" Holman asked.

"Don't know."

"Pay will be good. You will have meals and Boyo will be your assistant. He is a good boy. You will be in charge of feeding, training and preparing them for fights. You will have freedom to do anything you want in handling the birds...you can organise a new schedule if you wish."

They stood in the middle of the shed undernaeth a bank of flourescent lights. Around them there were sacks of corn, oats, bags of grits and specially mixed grain packed off the floor on ramps. In the open cupboards stood rows and rows of phials, large bottles, small demijohns, packages of tablets, boxes of disposable gloves and cartons of syringes, each item serving a special purpose in training and maintaining the health of Holman's fighting cocks. It was an impressive place.

"So, what you say?" Holman asked again.

"Deal," Moro agreed.

The rigid programme of training began and continued over the next twelve months. Moro would arrive long before dawn, a new twist in the bundle of hair at the back of his head and the faint smile of a man never in a hurry turning up the corners of his mouth. One after the other, the twelve cocks took turns alighting on to his leather-wrapped forearm to take their dose of medicine before beginning the exercises. Each bird was allotted a specific amount of time for its feed and exercise on the pole, then Moro would hold each one on his lap to rub down its head and neck, massaging the strong thighs and chest with brandy and ginger. Gently, sweetly, he caressed them and spoke to them as they bent their necks to take the grains he offered in his palm.

Then, after months of training, it was time. Holman stepped into the yard and hollered, "Moro, next Saturday, man. Hear them Cubans and Spaniards coming...and you can guess who...."

"El Diablo, boss?"

"Right. Think we have a chance, Moro? Think Trinidad might finally be in the picture?"

"Time'll tell, boss," Moro answered.

"Well, you are the trainer. You should know."

"Boss, dem oversea cocks is world-class, but dat doh mean a thing. A good fighter cock could come from de bush. Get what ah say?"

"Well, De Pas and Vasquez will be there."

"Let them come, boss. We go be there too!"

Early the next Saturday, they followed the winding road that took them through overgrown weeds into a mushy path of ruts and hoofprints. The black sticky mud made the journey perilous for the station wagon filled with stacked cages of fighting cocks.

They arrived long before daybreak, but they were not the first. There were others, consumed by anxiety and over-whelmed by their passion for action, who had long been camped beneath the forest shade. Green tents were pegged to the ground scout-style, and their own cages of birds were under careful watch as they awaited the beginning of the first contest.

The gayelle shimmered in the slow-rising sun, its small enclosure of sand encircled by the seats made of rough-hewn planks. At the side was the cubicle for the trainers, who held their birds in small cages, the officials and the bettors. On the far side, the foreigners, mostly Spanish-speaking people, clenched foul-smelling cigars between chubby fingers ringed with gold.

Holman leaned close to Moro to whisper in his ear, "That's Malaban over there in the Panama hat. See his big moustache? More hair in it than feathers on the birds he breeds. That man has killers."

"El Diablo is the one we have to watch, boss," Moro said.

"Think Satan will make it?"

"He have a chance. He jumping good these days."

In minutes the gayelle blossomed into a riotous blaze of hot-pink shirts, fancy hats and black spectacles worn on sweaty foreheads, as if to compete with the colourful plumage of the game cocks. The contest began quickly. The barricade bent forward under the strain of the pressing crowd which craned over in an effort to see the fighting cocks in action.

The first fight was brief. There was a flurry of feathers, sharp beaks and bloody spurs punctuated by the loud voices of those who bet and lost. Someone swore in Spanish, a bottle of mountain dew changed hands, and more notes were peeled off thick wads from waistcoat pockets. Five local birds, two of the best from Malgrétoute, succumbed to the spurs of the foreign champions and were soaked in their own blood. They were destroyed by sheer speed and power, the like of which had never been seen from the local fighters. Then, the long-awaited moment arrived. The battler with an unbeaten record, the king of cocks, the terrible killer came into the ring. El Diablo.

By this time the crowd had swelled and the trainers had taken their cocks into the gayelle. Moro stood with Satan, the bird black and gleaming in the sunlight, a wild look in its eyes as it scratched the sand with its feet. El Diablo stood its ground fearlessly, the long tail curving in an arch of brilliant red, touching the sand far behind. Its head was almost flat at the top; its strong, pointed beaks were nearly as sharp as its pair of deadly spurs which had been chiselled to a fine point.

The cocks flew and clawed at each other in the ring. As Satan jumped into the air, both feet pumped with mechanical efficiency. Landing on its feet, it soared again, driving its spurs ahead.

Ready for battle, the great Spanish bird retaliated. True to its name it recoiled instantly and dived under its opponent, keeping low to the ground as the clatter of spurs echoed overhead and the flapping of wings churned the sand around.

"Caramaba," a Spaniard muttered as the others puffed on their cigars and laughed.

El Diablo rushed forward in a red rage, attacking in strong thrusts with its beak, but Satan had long moved its head in fast feinting movements until they flew up together in a clash of feathers. Again the pumping legs, the curved half-open deadly beaks – and this time blood spattered on the sand.

They rose and clashed again and again, beaks digging into reddened flesh, bloody spurs stabbing in a flurry of attack. Feathers were scattered over the ground and tossed about by the breeze. El Diablo wheeled around, its head so low it nearly touched the ground. Satan fired its spurs once, but the Spanish bird was too fast. It soared in the air in one jump as if prodded by some mysterious force, and its feet tore into the neck and head of the black opponent. Satan crumpled, drenched in blood, as the mutterings of the crowd rose. El Diablo rushed in for the kill, a twisted mass of beak and spurs, pouncing on to the writhing form of Satan stretched out in the dust.

Holman jumped into the arena to gather up his bird. A Spaniard leaned forward and caught El Diablo, to pat its head. He kissed El Diablo's red comb, smoothed its feathers and lifted the wings to examine the bird for wounds. The cries of the foreigners rose above the crowd.

With just three victories to the Trinidadians, they acknowledged defeat. There was an aggressiveness in the foreign birds which could never be found in their own cocks. Holman recognised the superiority and fighting instincts in the five cocks from Haiti and Martinique, and knew there was a strong need for more training and breeding to develop a better fighting strain.

He turned away from the gayelle, Satan in his arms. The bird was bloodied and dying from deep lacerations over its head, neck and breast. He jostled out of the trainers' cubicle, into the open, and looked about.

"Where is Moro?" he asked under his breath.

The deafening voices of the Cubans and Spaniards rose

afresh as they began their celebration. It was then that Moro appeared, slowly walking into the arena, the plait of hair at the back of his neck and the slight smile on his spice-coloured cheeks. Perched on his forearm, its feet clasping on to leather, was a red and black Dom. It stood tall, its head almost round, but it had no tail.

"Thought you left us, Moro."

"No, boss. I know that El Diablo was too good for us."

"Where you got that bird?"

"This is one ah mine own. I bring two cocks just in case. This one good boss."

"You entering that?"

"Yes, only way to know. Nothing to lose."

Holman smiled as he scrutinised the cock on Moro's arm. It was odd-looking with its large, round head and the stump of short feathers behind. Once in the arena, the tailless bird evoked laughter from the crowd. It was weighed, and someone remarked about going back home for its clothes, but Moro stood his ground proudly. He patted the bird's back, speaking encouraging words as if the cock could understand what he was saying.

In the gayelle, El Diablo stood like a pillar of fire, red down to its toes. Groomed afresh, its eyes burned for more blood, the loud cackle from its throat rattling like a chac-chac shaken after a victory. The Spaniards threw their hats into the sand, and clouds of cigar smoke drifted across the gayelle.

Again there was laughter at the tailless Trinidad bird, though it stood taller than the red Spanish terror. It even drew a smile from the Trinidad crowd, though they had suffered their fifth straight defeat at the hands of the foreigners.

Sand and loose feathers torn from the underside of El Diablo flew when the fighting cocks began their battle. The betting resumed, though many were hesitant to place their money on the Trinidad fighter. El Diablo was the red menace, conqueror from overseas, the one always victorious.

In a flash, El Diablo whirled around thrusting its spurs with deadly accuracy, but Tailless counter-attacked, springing higher as they clashed in the air. When they landed, Tailless had already planted four strokes on El Diablo's head, and a hush fell over the Spaniards, who looked amazed. Again, the barricades bent forward under the pressing weight of the crowd. Holman edged closer to Moro. Moro remained cool, pensive, watchful.

Driven into a greater frenzy, El Diablo charged again. At first it kept its head very low, crawling along the ground like a snake, dodging from side to side, holding the crowd spellbound with its crafty wile. A murmur of surprise rose from the foreigners upon seeing the true mettle of their great fighter. They whispered to one another, as El Diablo renewed its terrifying assaults. Tailless retreated from the stabbing spurs that had already ripped across an unguarded chest, blood spewing off its flanks onto the sand.

El Diablo flapped its wings and bounded into the air. With a drop of its mighty head, its beak found the target in the underside of its adversary.

Then it happened. El Diablo retreated, low on the ground, thrusting its head forward, wings unfolded, as it prepared to leap again. Tailless waited, and when they rose, El Diablo had already torn into the exposed thighs of the Trinidad bird. Feathers blew across the arena, and the Spaniards chuckled around their fat cigars.

It was only when the flapping wings were folded and the cocks landed from their short flight that they saw the pointed spur sticking through the neck of El Diablo.

"Look!" someone shouted.

"Mammá miá," a Spaniard gasped.

Holman looked closely, as the sand around the cocks reddened. El Diablo fluttered, then stretched out in the throes of defeat. It attempted to flap its once-proud plumage, tarnished by its own sticky gore. The crowd jumped to its feet, and someone rushed into the ring. Another dived in to pull Tailless away as it pounced on the fallen cock to pick at its victim's eyes.

Moro gently lifted Tailless into his arms, caressing his bird. As he lifted its wings, a gasp escaped his throat when he felt his hands moistened. Furtively, he turned away clutching his bird deep into his chest.

It was sudden pandemonium as everyone pushed into the arena. In the uproar, someone picked up El Diablo, its mouth wide open, the head and neck wet with blood that oozed from its wounds.

Holman smiled. His own people hugged him in congratulation. They jumped the barricades into the arena to slap him on the back for winning the most important fight of the season. At last they had produced a great champion, gaining the prestigious Caribbean title for the first time in the history of the games. To Holman and his fellow trainers, it meant that they had arrived at a milestone in the sport, and that with dedication and continuous training and breeding, they would be able to produce their own successful strain. Moro had proved that by entering his tailless battler, which he had raised in his own yard. With his expertise and Holman's excellent facilities, they knew they would make a great team.

"No more Venezuelan cocks," Moro heard someone say. "Just now we goh do we own exporting."

"Never see a cock fight so yet," another remarked. "Imagine if he had a tail!"

Alcohol flowed in celebration. Then Holman moved out of the enclosure and turned toward the trainers. He looked over their heads, into the faces of the foreigners, once again searching for Moro. He had disappeared, as before, into the crowd.

Holman elbowed and pushed, trying to edge his way out of the crowd that held him back to shake his hand and congratulate him. He asked everyone he met on his way out if they had seen Moro. Finally, he shook the hand of a man who said he had seen someone leave the gayelle alone, his hair plaited at the back of his head, walking in a peculiar shuffle.

"He was walking straight ahead without looking back. About five minutes now. Look, he gone up de road," the little man explained. "He have a dead fowl cock in he hand that ent have no tail."

Six O'Clock Special

Dawn broke quietly through the rustle of palms. The cane arrows were gently swaying to morning winds when the mother stirred in her kitchen and doused the glowing embers of firewood. She had risen earlier than usual.

Blue smoke from the chula crept and curled into the dingy bedroom, making her son cough. But he too was long up. He tossed the torn flour-bag bedding aside, slipped quickly into trousers, a pair of which the mother had selected for him the afternoon before. He drew a towel over his shoulders, he shivered and stooped before the still warm chula. Through the kitchen window, patches of dasheen, freshened by dew drops, stood against the background of blacksage and bull grass. The brown, stagnant swamp remained a formidable barrier to the savannah lands.

"Mamoo going wid us too?" the boy asked. He stared into the last dim spark in the ashen hearth. The mother, making busy movements at the fireside, answered softly: "When he done tie his cattle, beta. Take the datwan and wash you mouth quick."

"Pa staying wid us?" he asked again.

"That train special coming in the station for half hour only, beta. And is because they fixing the train line. Dat is what Mr Woodley say. So is the last chance to see your Pa."

"That train does be full a workman, Ma. It goh be late! Tomorrow is Christmas."

They ate in silence, the sada roti still warm in their hands. After the meal the mother crouched with her enamel teacup over a low wooden bench near the doorway so that she could throw bits of roti to the fowl that were coming down the high branches of the chataigne tree.

"Why he not staying, Ma? He gone so long from us," the son asked, huddled in the shadows. But the mother, not answering his question, said instead: "Hurry now beta, it getting late. Mr Woodley looking out for we soon."

"Who he? The station master?"

"And when you see your Pa doh make him fret. Doh steups and talk chupidness. You know how he temper is? Bad like yours."

When they had eaten, the mother poked the fire and poured coconut oil from a bottle she took down from the low carat ceiling. She rubbed her hands, then her arms and legs. After wiping her face she wiped her hands on the boy's head and cheeks until they shone.

"Comb your head, beta. You must look good. Pa want to see you fresh and smart."

She looked deep into his eyes, cupping his face in her hands. Then she pushed his shirt into his trousers. She held him close to her chest for a long, long time.

Then the boy took his bird cage from where it hung in the kitchen and came out to meet his mother. "Doh take dat beta, we can't carry it and the cage weak."

"I want to show Pa dis bird, Ma. Is he catch it for me."

"No beta. Leave it. I have this pumpkin choka and roti. We will carry it for him. You know how long he eating dry bread?"

Out of the house, the mother pulled shut the crude wooden door and passed a chain around the doorpost. It was drizzling slightly. Hunching her shoulders the mother muttered "panee away la."

Almost two miles from the village junction, their little cottage was the last in line on that trace. Last on that trace because Poolool had wanted it that way. It stood alone in the wilderness, the swamps stretching out on one side to profuse shrubs over which grew calabash and wild cherries.

The forest attained a deeper green in the rainy season and shouldered cacao lands near a little brown river that snaked its way through the woods where the father used to take his son in search of river conchs.

Red-footed brown doves were already cooing amongst worms in the cashew patch when the mother came down the cobbled path holding the boy's hands at the inclince, where heaps of pebbles and twigs assailed them at the curve.

The sky brightened and the air was cool. The son never knew why he lived on that trace, so far from the other houses which were grouped higher up the road. But the mother knew the father as a man who kept always to himself and never liked mingling with people.

Almost reaching the junction, they went into the Mamoo's yard; the house, an unpainted wooden structure on balata stilts. The Mamoo came out and began talking quietly with the mother while the son stood in the yard. The boy stood uneasily and wondered why they spoke so long. His Mamoo stood on the last treaders of the stairway buttoning his shirt over his paunch and his mother, arms folded, looked up at his face.

"That six o'clock special train does come on Monday

only, but you sure it coming today? Dis is Christmas Eve, Dolly," the Mamoo asked when they were on his cart. He snapped his whip behind the mule.

"Yes, Mr Woodley tell me," the mother replied.

"I know they fixing the line and them by the changing point," the Mamoo said.

"I hope Pool will be on that special train," the mother raised her voice, but it was drowned by the rumbling wheels trundling into the hard ruts. The son, grasping a corner post of the cart, sat with one hand around his mother, their backs to the mule; their legs dangled with the bucket under the cart.

The journey was rough along the stony road, the mother held on to her son in silence. The cane lands appeared, the tall palmiste trees lining the road on each side. They passed the pond and the rusty windmill, then the broken barracks and, in the open, the cane derrick. When they reached the slanting railway station, the mule swung to the right on a narrow track that ran to the side of a pile of railroad sleepers and a huge, whitewashed concrete cistern at the back of the building. People stood around barefooted, some in 'water washed' shirts, others dressed under felt hats, shirt sleeves rolled up to their elbows.

On the platform, the Mamoo, the mother and her son kept by themselves next to the huge signboard near the fencing which ran the full width of the platform area. The mother held her son's shoulders, leaning against the teak fence, and she appeared tense and nervous. She remained silent and stared at the two narrow, shining steel rails running over the oil-stained sleepers, her eyes unblinking as if she expected some catastrophe.

At first, they heard a slight rumble on the tracks that grew louder. Black and monstrous, the locomotive appeared coasting in, in all its heavy, chugging noise. The son nudged closer to the mother as the steam, hissing from under the engine, clouded the entire platform. Three grimy, liver-coloured metal carriages slowed to a stop with a clang of metal, followed by two sooty wooden carriages at the end of which was the enclosed goods wagon. The brake van was coupled last and from its jalousied window a man was looking out in his uniform and black cap.

"See if you see him, beta, you father," the mother goaded the son. Her eyes opened, her head making quick move-ments. The mother's hand tightened on the boy's shoulders and a new fierce spirit came out of her. The windows flashed before her and her frantic eyes searched for the familiar face of her husband.

The people that had gathered in the station looked at them. A few people were whispering; the channa vendor kept his distance. Short Mr Woodley, in rimless glasses, came out of the station dressed in khaki, even down to his cork hat. He greeted the mother and took the group to the special cubicle of the last carriage. Out of the narrow window, framed in expanding wire mesh and bars, the father looked out, his eyes large, brown and still. His lips parted slowly.

Pale, lean, his head was shaven but the stubble of beard covered his chin and fringed the wide, defiant mouth. At Mr Woodley's nod the guard opened the carriage door cau-tiously and the father came down the step, but his right hand was still fastened to another big man sitting inside the carriage. The Mamoo came up to the father, hugged him around the shoulder and patted him on his back. The mother came in a rush and buried her head in her husband's chest and almost collapsed. "Pool, what ah go do now?" she moaned. The father, regaining his posture, did not reply but stretched his hand and touched the boy's head instead. Then, one-handed, he embraced them for a long time. People on the platform stared curiously at them and the ticket collector had to knock on the gate with his pincers to call away the travellers. The son stood away from the father now, who looked tall and haggard as he spoke to him in his deep unaltering voice.

"Beta, you big now. Just now you is man. Listen to you Ma! You hear!" The boy shook his head but he remained silent.

"Answer you father, beta," the mother said, her wet cheeks shielded by the orhni.

The Mamoo enquired: "Why you didn't take Rammie as counsel. He get off Lalchan and Soogrim?"

"Who? Rammie Laumanth? Dat lawyer take my two cattle wid heifer, Sook. Is only opium-man he working for. He have money to build he house," the father replied.

"This case shoulda try in town. You know Rammie and dat judge is good pals. Dey woulda get you off, scotch free." The father shook his head.

"Done happen so, Sook, and ah not putting my little house and piece ah land to fight them."

"Ah tell you, Rammie have connection, he goh pull strings; he goh bring any amount ah witness. Dat is why he does win most ah de time."

"Is okay, Sook, ah go leave me land for me son, I done live my life ahready."

The father looked down, his face bland and sallow except for those large brown eyes. He turned to his son. "How the silverbeak bird? Singing sweet as yet?"

"A lil bit in the morning, Pa."

"Dat good. Just now he goh turn grey to old male, and den he will sing out he liver for you."

The boy only smiled. "Ma didn't want me to bring it."

"Take good care ah dat bird beta, the same way like you goh have to treat your Ma." He stretched out his left hand, gathered him once more against his body and rubbed his cheeks all over his son. He placed his hand on the boy's head. "Son, hear dis. Doh ever sell dat piece ah land even if the house bon down. Land is power, beta. Dat is all the power in dis world. Money and man does go, beta. But not land. It goh bear for you and your Ma. Your Nannie always say so. Me, Poolool, say so too."

But the son understood nothing, seeing that his father was a bit excited. He kept looking at his father. Then out of her tight throat the mother said: "Land is power. We go keep it." The Mamoo and the mother were also looking intensely at the father and were not distracted by other people in the carriage. Then a loud whistle blew.

"Thanks, Mr Woodley. Ah glad you bring dem. Is the last and I feel alright now," the father said. Mr Woodley only nodded his head.

"I did it for your Christmas, Pool. I knew the old man a long time now." The guard appeared and held the father's arms to lead him up the step into the carriage. The mother lunged forward, a shrill cry came out of her mouth, but the guard kicked out his leg to block her path. The Mamoo came up quickly from behind, grasped the mother around her waist and dragged her backwards, her hands and legs flailing wildly. The guard turned the brass handle of the carriage door, then the father pressed his face to the wire mesh and said, "Is the only way, Dolly. Take care ah the boy. Have a nice Christmas, all yuh. Doh worry bout me."

"All you watch the foot board, m'am. The train moving out now," the guard cautioned. The platform cleared. The porters pushed the barrows under the awnings of the goods shed. Raising his arm high the guard turned, faced the engine driver and shook the green flag vigorously. The engine was steaming up, billowing smoke spurted out of the chimney; it blew its loud steam whistle. Through the expanding metal of the carriage window the father looked outside for a long time at the three people in his life. The mother held her son around the shoulders, one hand covered her mouth with the orhni. As she looked into the carriage she saw the widened eyes of her husband, round and as brown as nutmegs, set on his face without expression or emotion. The carriages moved out, slowly at first, then gathered speed as the engine chugged forward and the whole train left the station at a quickening pace. The sky was darkened by dense black smoke.

The Mamoo went behind the station where the cart was tied, but the mother stood motionless on the deserted railway platform.

Then the boy, looking up to his mother, asked: "When Pa coming back home?" But the mother neither answered, nor lowered her head.

Rikhi's Statement

I name is Rikhi Poolool. I is nine years old and I live in Carolina. Pa dead after Ma the same week and I know what happen: it clear as rain water. And days after before they carry Bunty away in the police van, he hold me face in he two hands and say, "Rikhi, is you alone now, boy. Take care. I going for I don't know how long. If I doh see you again, remember one thing, you must do what you mind say. You hear me? Be brave and remember what Ma used to say sometime, she was too good to us, boy." Yet talking to me he looking far away and I know he didn't want me to see he face. Before he coulda say anything more the police pull he away and shove he in the van, he two hand handcuff, barefoot, mud stick up all over he tear-up pants and he look like he come from some hole in the ground.

I walk home, Bunty face twist up in pain behind the wire window in the van still in my mind. I feel the whole world cant down. Until I reach the trace that pass through the burial ground. I look to see if I coulda still see Ma grave with the bunch a bright flowers on top it. I feel as if I drain down to the ground. I weak, weak, weak.

"Be brave," Bunty say but he was brave too and look how he end up. I say to myself some people does do brave things but they does always end up lock up. Like Kumar. He break down the estate store room and take rum and he get a long jail for that. Ramsook thief molasses and he get lock up too.

But the worst was Blacks. He kill the overseer because he get short pay and the police shoot he in the coconut where he was hiding for four days.

Them was the days in the village when sadness like a black rain cloud used to drop from the sky and stifle me. You can't breathe and nobody sorry for me until as if that cloud buss and bring all that water from my eye wetting up me knee and I taste salt.

I begin to see Ma in the field with bag a salt, throwing it around in the ground. "Coming, Beta," she used to say, and I stooping down under the immortelle tree in the shade, was pinching the alloo from the sada roti she have wrap up in the flour bag towel.

Them was the days she hold me to her breast in that hot sun, when as soon as school over, I run to meet she in the canefield. I smell that Ma closeness in she and that good old sweat, warm and wet like pound jeera and coconut oil. Oil she used to massage my body when I have fever and I lay down on the ground on bag to sleep, rain dancing over my head and the galvanise rattling like stone talking.

Ma was always talking about leaving people thing alone. "Doh bring home anybody mango and thing from they yard," she say. And Bunty grow up something like she. He take after she because thirsty like hell and he own friend offer he a press with milk and he ent taking it.

Them was the days too when I sense something wasn't right home because Pa used to quarrel so much. Beating Ma and kicking she in she belly. I used to cry holding my head and hiding under the flour bag blanket. He used to drink. Cussing and spitting all over the house and talking so hard them neighbour, Chachee and Chacha Balraj used to get fed up, looking through they window in the night.

Ma used to talk to he easy. Talking about something that she didn't like. I really didn't know what was going on, but in the middle ah the night they still talking. Pa getting vex, Ma crying. And then it happen.

One night the door knock. Ma say, "Who dat?" And before she light the flambeau to open the door, I see Pa put on he pants quick and jump through the window. Two black policeman stand up by the door, the button on they shirt shining and they have bootoo in they hands. I hear Mamoo dog barking and I know is Pa running in the trace to the canefield.

Them police come in, dig up the house with they bootoo. They open the rice box and chook up the dhan, flash they torchlight all over the room, the light fall on the old bedding on the ground. In the kitchen they open the pot and stir up the fireside. When they gone, I could still smell them, strong like mule pee.

Bunty was only eighteen but he was big. He leave school in third standard because he want to work. He used to tote me on he back, and we used to run away and go by the trainline, looking for cane and picking up molasses that drip on the line and suck it. He grow up with he own mind, Ma say. One thing he did used to like Ma a lot. The first work he get in the estate was riding trace mule. He used to bring the money to Ma. "Be straight," he used to always tell me, "If is one thing doh touch people thing."

The real trouble start when Ma get sick. She start to spit blood and Pa take her to the estate doctor. He used to come only on Friday in a old box car and Ma had to wait long days before she see him. The tablets he give her didn't work because she get worse and Pa get worried. Then for days, for weeks, he had to stay home. He lose days and the estate didn't give him any pay for that. The estate even wanted to fire him because he was staying home so much.

It was a funny thing with Pa, one minute he vex, voice like thunder, trampling and shaking up the house like a bad bull in a pen. The next minute he cool like melon, quiet like stone. Sitting on the doorstep and picking lice from Ma head.

That is why he must be feel that he had to get Ma to the doctor to get she better. He feel somehow the licks she get from he when he drunk must be cause she to spit blood. And all that come from money. Money. The fortnight pay was never enough for Pa to drink rum with. To run the house Ma used to get three dollars. Some days we didn't have milk or oil. Nothing save up and when Ma had to see a special doctor in town it was more trouble because that doctor was calling for plenty money.

But long before that, as I say, I know that something wasn't right in the house. Like the night when Kumar come to meet him. That was before he make the two years in prison. I hear them talking quiet in the gallery. It was moonlight night. I peep through the crack in the window and I hear them talking about estate payday, Friday.

It wasn't Kumar alone. Ramsook was Pa friend too and no surprise, Blacks. The bravest man in Carolina. He sell he mother cow when she ask he to change it in the Savannah. Since he small he in this wickedness; picking Nanny plums, carrying she ducks to the market. One time he and Ramsook sell two Estate Farmal wheel to a man in Bronte. After that they spree for one whole month. Another time they cart away a load a sugar one night and sell it to a shopkeeper in Balmain. The police never catch them but they all say Pa had a hand with them.

"See what your Ma want, Rikhi," Pa used to say as he sit down looking into the road that twist for miles like a horse whip snake between rows and rows a cane. The sun beat down like a big lantern until the road smoke and them dead crapaud smoking like overcook saheena frying in oil. Mule cart and bison winding down the road creaking with load with froth melting like lard in them Zebu mouth.

I know how Pa feel. Because with all that short temper and mountain dew mouth and all that set a licks he does give, he could be like a dove sometime.

It was Bunty who I didn't know coulda be really so brave. Maybe it was Pa fault that Bunty had to listen. Sankar was lock up, Blacks done bury in the burial ground and Ramroop in jail too. So Pa want help. He carry Bunty that Friday in the cane under the culvert that stand up by the bend in the road.

The paymaster was riding he mule and they cut he down like grass, the animal fall dead, Mr Collins was too old to stand up after all them blows. He hit he head on the ground and he ears bleed and he head turn like a buss water melon that fall from a cart. The water carrier who was coming behind see and run back to the factory. And in no time them police come down the road.

They shoot Pa like a dog in the mang, the knapsack over he shoulder with all them notes wet up in the mud because rain fall that day. When they find he the police carry me to see if he was my Pa. Two fly sit down right on he forehead, he two eye open looking up as if asking for help. But I know it wasn't that, because Pa is not the kinda man to ask for help. He too proud, too different. It was Ma he was thinking about and the medicine. But she pass away all the same just after they shoot he. The news kill she and when she hear Bunty hiding, that make it worse.

Rain was falling bucket a drop and the mule cart tote Pa body out, he head hanging down behind, he eye still wide open as if he watching who following he to the station.

It take them three days before they get the body, Mamoo and Rookmin and them, and by the time they ready to bury he swell up. Nobody, not even we neighbour come to the funeral and the pundit say he too busy. But I know everybody shame. So Mamoo, Chacha Babraj and two creole mista who working in the tractor shed come and help put down the box. We bury him in the next lot where all them hang man does bury, the place full a grass and them calabash tree standing up right there. Only them black Merle-corbeaux weighing down the branch black and bawling as if they sorry for Pa going down in that deep hole. That was the only prayers.

After two days the police bring home Bunty to pick up a soap and comb and some clothes. They catch he by the ravine soaking in the mud, that same place he used to carry me for conchs.

This evening he talk to me for the last, not looking in my face, he looking away far, so that maybe I can't see he face, far where them cane shaking they leaf in the wind, where the dust spinning over them in the sun. The sun shining bright like some witness in the sky who does see all but doh say nothing. This is all I know and this is what I write. Me, Rikhi Poolool.

Death at Coramandel

At Coramandel, for seven days, he watched from the beach. The beach on which, three years later, his entrails and head would roll to the beaks and claws of carrion crows.

He saw the span of wrinkled sand, gleaming with naked holiday-makers tanning beneath the sky. The peak of his cap pointed out from behind the mangrove, his eyes furtively scanning the laze of brown legs, tummies and the flap of coloured towels lifting with the sea breeze that blew inland.

It was like the night – twelve Augusts ago – one of those months when Slinger beached his cargo of noisy birds and morocoys that sat on the covered shipment of packaged marijuana, the first batch of which had come on shore with Balbosa exactly five days before in his Venezuelan pirogue. As he grinned, Balbosa stood with the ponderous copper-chained medallion dangling over his broad chest. He had the effect of making some turn their eyes towards the horizon, while others pulled their salty caps over their faces whenever he levelled his poignard at their throats.

This fearsome incident was usually carried out in the middle of the Gulf, after which Balbosa would dump the bodies overboard, the heads.following separately with startled eyes, still unclosed, the stream of gore splashing the starboard around the poop house, where the splatter of blood would be washed with calabashes of sea water dipped by his own men. Now stooped over coconut husks, he waited with that calm, stoic patience, chain smoking, biting the ends of nutgrass and watching the parade of bachacs toting their loads of green leaves up trunk.

Then one afternoon a sail appeared. A dot of white on the horizon. The beach was desolate, the bathers having long retreated into the bath houses, shielding them from the traffic on the winding road which ran beneath the drooping lianes and purple orchids high overhead, where wild pines bristled in their etiolated gamboge pattern of yellows and ochres and where, too, the towering walls of teak and balata struggled upwards in a race with immortelles. The gloom and mustiness sprouted ferns and lichens, long dampened by the slanting rain.

But these never hampered the operations of the drug runners, whether it was in daytime or in the darkest nights. They would come out with the merchandise strapped over the motorcycles, or loaded in the land cruisers, escorted by their own men who searched out ambushers hiding in the forest thickets bordering the road or in the banana patches where the men hid beneath the broad leaves, dressed in green.

And that was the colour of the enemy; the green berets and corduroys, green T shirts, green socks. Even green faces appeared through the rousseau huts constructed as check points, deep in the forests where the cultivation of marijuana was carried out under the watchful eyes of shrewd planters, who selected the sheltered valleys behind thick undergrowth and marsh lands that made detection and access almost impossible.

Now the sail disappeared. But the dot of boat grew in size as the engines took over and the chugging was muffled by the onrushing waves and the cries of hovering gulls in the skies. It was a customary sight to see these gulls over the small boats, loaded with the shrimps of two sizes, conchs and waccoos dug out of the Venezuelan beaches, and jumbo crabs that found themselves on the plates of high-class restaurants where gourmets booked their table in advance for their appointments with agents.

Once ashore, the engine of the boat died as if with the fading rays of the sun, and by dusk, after the anchor had long bitten into the ooze of dead mangrove leaves, the water was bailed out from the boat in that routine manner after fishing trips.

Nightfall. On the lonely beach the men moved about with an air of triumph.

Discarding only their tight jerseys, they braced themselves to off-load the oblong compressed packets – an opaque white in daylight in cellophane cubes – but now pale yellow under the flambeau, held aloft so that the packages could be checked and neatly stacked into the jeep and station wagon concealed in the camouflage of undergrowth. Secret spots were chosen, different for each shipment, in order to avoid detection and the curiosity of the nearby villagers who led their train of cows and sheep through the narrow dirt tracks of the sleepy countryside.

"Cinquento, Señor Holman."

When the last seven packets were taken off the pirogue, he scrawled his name on the dotted line at the bottom of a sheet of paper. He wrote, as the Spaniard had always indicated to him, in accordance with the wishes of Sanchez: the name must be written twice, next to the quantities received, alongside his signature.

"Adios," and the Spaniard was gone.

He stood like an extension of the bow, carved in the same wooden, inert immobility, clutching the paper in his hand, while his men busied themselves with the engines that sputtered and coughed out of the shallows as they headed back to the border. Meanwhile the land cruiser and station wagon, weighed down over stretched springs, filtered out of the undergrowth. Zig-zagging, lights low with Mukesh at the wheel of the first vehicle, they headed for Piparo, Tortuga, and then to Tabaquite and Bois Jean Jean, where other vehicles were hidden in shady cocoa groves.

There too, men like Mazay, Koon and Dhole remained a way off, sitting in their own chauffeured vehicles, under the clothy veil of towels around their shoulders, hats pulled low over their foreheads, as they checked out the money. Blue and mauve bundles held by rubber bands, edges soaked with spittle, smelling as pungent as the acrid, weedy smoke that puffed out of their nostrils, clouding over the sacks in which Magnums and Colts were holstered. Underseat, the curved blades of poignards – specially brought in with Moroccan handles – embedded with ivory, like the metallic pearl butts of firearms, matched in fine style.

Then there came suddenly the record of facts, dealing with the circumstances, unravelling the evidence and revealing the details that led up to the finding of the white Mazda. Its battery was dead, four flat tyres had been slashed and it lay squat on the sand, surrounded by empty beer and soft drink cans and paper plates soiled brown from stains of half-eaten pelau, bottles and paper cups. The mangy, roaming hulks of emaciated pot hounds gnawed at the littered bones and left overs in preference to the corpse – a bloated, grotesque torso bereft of its head which rotted some distance off. The police dragged the corpse onto the plastic stretchers and into the waiting police van which quickly reversed out of the slosh and followed the other vehicles in military fashion out of the district.

That was how the remains of Holman, drug king, controversial police informer and ruthless smuggler were scooped away. He had perished in the high-stakes game. He had gambled and lost, leaving the stench of death trailing through the sleepy districts that November evening, when the fowl of the village had already alighted on the low branches of the pomerac and chulas had long begun to blaze under tawas sizzling with hot oil and garlic, at Coramandel.

Kimbo

He came into the village – as if from nowhere, one Sunday. Bastahall basked in April sunlight; men played cards under the shade of samaan and the stray dogs had slunk into the shadows.

It was crop time, the time of fierce sun. The air was sweet from the syrupy smell of sugar and fermenting molasses. Bisons groaned under loads of sugar cane, frothed at their mouths, strained under the biting, snapping whips of meagre boys perched aloft on their torsos.

He called himself Kimbo. But they knew it was his prison name and they suspected that he had come from another remote district high up the hills where the valley ran greener, into deep rivers.

Kimbo arrived, with a small bundle under his arm, in that carefree manner, in long loose strides for he was tall. The pantaloons clung tight over powerful thighs and his calves bulged. His head looked larger because of the mop of curly hair which fell over his neck. But his eyes were watery, white agates, round and gentle.

Along the estate road he passed the huge water tank, elevated over its iron pipe support and the paymasters' office in the clearing, with its white-washed wall, wooden enclosures and the trodden cane stalks scattered in the yard. Lower down he passed the cluster of houses, their shallow galleries crowded with potted plants and bag hammocks. Two women were busy washing over their tubs. Kimbo nodded at them but they only stared at him long and hard.

An empty cane cart came up the road, its tray rattling over the ruts, raising a cloud of dust. The cartman stood on the cart with the reins coiled around his wrists. When Kimbo raised his hands, he pulled his reins and the cart stopped.

"Where you going?" the man asked.

"The Barracks," Kimbo replied.

"Why?"

"Ross send me."

"You sure about that, man?"

"Yea, man. I have the key."

The man did not reply. He looked at Kimbo carefully and began to show a silent displeasure. Tugging at his reins, he hollered at the mule which trotted off, leaving Kimbo in another wake of dust. Kimbo watched the cart as it disappeared into the distance.

The sugar factory came up with its tall stack looming before him. His heart leapt at the sight of the factory compound, the buildings cloaked in an aura of rumbling machinery, hissing steam and the chugging locomotives shunting carriages on rails. He stood in amazement at the number of loaded cane carts awaiting the crane to hoist them onto the conveyor. Here, the smell of sugar was even stronger. Thick smoke rose out of the chimney stack and darkened the road.

He continued on his way until the macadam coating of the factory road gave way to loose gravel, then dirt, as the road narrowed at the bend, taking him between fields of cane. A torturous path descended slowly into a terrain of savannah grass and more rolling cane lands. The entrance came up before the low-lying spread – the sugar estate barracks.

He passed the fence of split teak saplings and barbed wire, and wondered who would meet him in this sprawling compound. The coppers were like giant bowls, next to the heaps of broken casks and cartons. Debris of useless cane carts and the litter of household junk stood out in the yard in mounds piled among the random sprouts of grass. Children played unmindful of his entrance.

Kimbo entered the second entrance and searched for No. 117. Two women were shelling peas. Further down another was feeding her chickens. He looked in their direction but they did not notice that he had entered the barrack yard. From where he stood he saw numerous little entrances, each leading up to a small enclosed space before steps and a door. The whole structure was a powdery white that broke in patches of various hues of greys and browns. He walked down the long unpaved yard, hard and stony, where clothes were spread out on the bleaches.

He found No. 117 five doors down, mounted the two steps, felt for a key and entered. There was only one window. He opened it and sunlight blazed on the floor in one square patch. Dust motes rose and streamed in clouds. On the floor were two iron pots, discarded enamel plates, a cup and yellowing newspapers. In the corner was a small wooden table worn shabby from use and age, its top unpainted like the loose boards assembled on the elevated stand that stood for a bed. The corners of the room were littered with empty bottles and cigarette butts. It smelt of tobacco and urine. Kimbo dumped his bundle on the make-shift bed, but before he could open it he heard a loud rapping at the door. Surprised, he turned to see three men in the small cubicle space at his steps.

"Sure you in the right place, man?" The question came

from the man on the steps, bulky as a bison, leaning his massive body on the door frame. Another stood behind him with his chest exposed, his red shirt unbuttoned. It hung loosely on his shoulders, knotted around his waist. The third appeared two paces behind, but he seemed implanted in the yard like some ancient headstone carved out of ebony, his hands behind his back. He said nothing, but kept staring at Kimbo.

"Yeah," Kimbo said.

"How you know?" the big man asked.

Kimbo showed him the key and the man laughed. A slow rattle came out of his throat as he looked back at his two companions.

"Look, you better find out. Mr Ross ent have right to give out rooms like this," he said.

And pointing his finger into Kimbo's face he added, "Yuh better check with he again, man. We doh know you in the fuss place."

Kimbo kept looking at his key. He twirled the metallic ring in his hands.

"Must be a mistake," Kimbo said.

"You making the mistake, pal," the man insinuated. He shifted his foot a little inside the room and waited.

Kimbo looked over his head at the other two men. The one that looked squat like a tombstone stared back at Kimbo. He was silent.

"What you doing?" the man at the door asked. The man behind him muttered under his breath, "Tell the man he can't stay."

He had his right hand under his shirt and he kept it there all the time, while the other behind him kept his hands behind his back, looking on, the white of his eyes fixed in one direction.

Kimbo turned to get his bundle from the bed and came down the steps, locking the door behind him. He thought there was no harm in checking with Mr Ross, but it would have to be on Monday. It was only when Kimbo reached the gate out of the compound that the third man moved. His hands were clasped around the handle of a long poignard he held, thrust into his pants behind his back.

The next morning Kimbo arrived at Mr Ross' office. The factory compound was busy with men around their carts which were left propped up for the weekend. The roads were crowded.

He was surprised to meet the same three men who had visited him the day before coming out of Mr Ross' office. They passed, glaring at him. One remarked "You win, this time pal!"

When Kimbo came out of Mr Ross' office his face was brightened, and there was a new bounce in his step. He passed the men loitering at the junction near the small lean-to shed at the guard hut. As he reached the hut, he felt an uneasiness and caught in the corner of his eyes the shuffle of feet. He heard one of them cough, a slow dragging cough as if he was clearing his throat. The ball of phelgm sailed over his head, landing on the wall of the hut.

"Damn chamar," a voice muttered behind him.

Kimbo felt his skin cool and the hairs on his neck rise with a strange knifing spasm that ran through his body. But he kept on in that same unhurried stride, carefree and loose-limbed, and his eyes were as wet as always and as gentle as dew drops. He kept at an even pace until he reached the gate which came like a marking point for the detonating explosion. The bottle shattered against the culvert, its fragments rained around him. Two more bottles fell before him but Kimbo kept his cool, and neither stopped nor quickened his pace.

Kimbo, now found himself at nights confined in the one-room apartment reeking of grime and squalor. He spent his work days in the stench of the mule pens. He fed the animals, cleared the pens and took care of the feeble mules who were too old for strenuous work. He took time off to shop in the village and in the afternoons cooked his bully beef over an open fire near the copper. Some days he slept in the stock room, sprawled over sacks of oatmeal, or immersed in bundles of grass piled high in the cow shed.

One day he worked late and stayed in the pen. The next afternoon, when he went home, he was surprised to meet people standing at his door. Some held their nostrils and backed away and Kimbo himself was startled by the foul smell which came from his room. He opened the door and the stench was stronger. When Kimbo entered he saw on his dilapidated bed the rotting carcass of a dog. He never again stayed overnight in the estate after work.

Two weeks passed. Kimbo came home late in the afternoons, boiled his pot of tea in the cubicle outside, and sat on the doorstep because of the stifling dry season heat.

One night he arrived to find the same three men who tried to evict him standing in the yard. Two stood in the darkness and the bison-like man was on his doorstep.

"So you still here, man?" the bison-man said.

"Leh we finish he, Ganga," the second man said as they both came out of the shadows and stood around Kimbo. He saw the sticks in their hands. Ganga, the bison-man, held a cutlass.

"We doh want no chamar here. You know that? So how come you doh get the message?"

Kimbo looked at him, felt the rage knotting in the bottom of his stomach. His lips twitched but he remained silent. Windows in the barracks opened and light from kerosene lamps fell on the yard in small bright patches. People were singing lower down the barrack yard, and a voice rose over the tuneless medley of folk songs.

"Hi ya neighbour, wha going on and so late, Kim?" It was Nella, a dougla who had become a close friend of Kimbo since he moved in. She was dry-boned and loose-hipped; she had a special liking for Kimbo's rambling stride and had fallen for his liquid eyes. She craned her neck out of the darkness.

But Kimbo's mind was far away from those leisurely moments of song and celebration taking place in the barrack yard not more than twenty yards away. He heard tinkling glasses and the wild eruptive laughter.

"Anything wrong Kim?" The cheery-toned voice rose above the melee. It was Nella's voice again.

Kimbo did not answer. Nella's voice had distracted the attention of Ganga and the man standing at his side. It was at that very moment Kimbo sprang into action, becoming in that split second a demon with flailing arms and legs. He dropped abruptly on his two hands and his feet shot out like ramrods. They struck Ganga full on his chest with such force that he was thrown against the wall of the barrack room. Heads rose in the lamp light. Kimbo jumped as if by some supernatural force, ascended with his long arms extended over his head, and when he had reached the full height of his jump, his feet shot out again like pistons. One black heel caught the second man full on his throat and he plummeted in a gargle of suppressed pain; the cutlass was thrown off.

But the man who had back-pedalled in the shadows now came out with his blade flashing. He swung his weapon in a carving, looping chop when Kimbo was still in the air, suspended by his own momentum.

The blade passed under his armpit in a humming sound, swished up in another deadly arc and, on its return, descended like a falling light as it caught the flambeaux glare. But Kimbo had long moved, ducking under it. Kimbo raised his knee under the man's stomach, held him by his throat as he turned, and pinned the man's hands with one twist behind his back. People came out half-dressed from the barrack rooms. Those drinking were the first to crowd over the fallen Ganga. They stood and watched, but Nella's voice rose above the commotion.

"All you leave the man alone, nah."

"Mind you business," Ganga complained.

"Why you don't go home – the man ent do all you one thing," she shouted, her hips rounded in the semidarkness, as she stood holding her rum glass before her.

"Woman, you fast. This is man business," one of the attackers said.

"You, whey all-you come from? Go back to all-you room, man. You come from the next barrack – quite down on the other side. What right you have here?" Nella asked.

Two months afterwards on a Saturday when the incident was almost forgotten, after the estate had given a bonus to the workers, a fête was given on the F row barrack yard. People brought out their crude wooden benches and placed them in a circle after sweeping the yard. Nella took out her cane-varnished chairs and centre table on which she added a bouquet of hibiscus and dahlia. On the side tables were flagons of sorrel, bottles of ginger beer, sugarcake and black sticky balls of toolom. A large pot boiled in the yard with pelau, a concoction of tasso, pigtail and peas.

The celebration was in full swing with music, food and drink being shared by all.

Out of the merriment, someone pointed to the glow of sparks ascending in the cool night sky beyond the rooftops. The music stopped and the gathering stood unsteadily on its feet. Someone shouted: "Fire".

Two benches turned over, a bucket of ice spilled. The quatro players threw their instruments in the gallery and tripped over two drunken men who had rolled under the chairs. Everyone dashed to the E row barrack compound.

The fire was crackling bright. Pandemonium. People ran towards the fire and then, feeling intense heat, returned in confusion. The fire was at the end of barrack F.

"O God, all my things inside there," a woman, her lips reddened with wine, bawled out, "O Lord, Frank inside!" Frank was her crippled son, who was maimed when a cart rolled over him in the canefield. She held her head and ran up to her door. But the red flames were lashing out, rising along the banister and walls. Helpless, people stood with their mouths open as the fire leapt up to the sky. It drifted with the wind and travelled along the walls to adjacent barrack rooms.

Some scampered for buckets and ran towards the pipe, a good distance away. Others turned to their water drums, half empty, their levels too low for dipping.

Another woman broke away and ran up to the steps of her room and fell. A man ran after her and dragged her out. Children were bawling, running in all directions. Another old woman wept, held her face and stooped on the ground to pray.

Most of the men were either too drunk or fearful of the heat to help prevent the fire from spreading. The women were becoming more frantic. Then out of the morass of helplessness, out of the barrack compound, a figure emerged, standing head and shoulders above the crowd. He seized a bucket of water from the busy hands around him and doused himself. The next bucket he took up to the burning wall and dashed it with full force. Then another against the other partition; and another and another. Soon they turned to pots, pans, old basins. The vessels changed hands and Kimbo organised them one at a time and splashed it against the flames. He had just returned from work.

Kimbo hurled himself against a door and it fell in a crash. He ran back to the line and took a bucket of water. Against the stifling smoke, he pitted his long arms, ignoring the falling lumber. Twice he fell inside the blazing inferno, his lanky frame seemed consumed by the bright flashes that lapped up the dry timber, but he emerged, taking the buckets and pouring them onto the fire.

The woman who had fainted got up again and asked for Frank, her son, who lived in the next room. Kimbo leapt into the blaze with another washbasin and disappeared under the collapsed lintels of the barrack room. For a long time he did not come out and they wondered, as the buckets piled up in the yard. But he appeared again, holding up someone on his shoulders at the other end of the barrack. He had emerged safely out of the flames with Frank, who, though smothered with smoke and burns, was safe.

Leaving the victim on the ground, Kimbo went to work again, carrying the basins of water and running back with the empties in an orchestrated movement, attacking the fire at the bases first, and then on the paths where it was advancing along the walls. He worked nonstop until the flames died little by little.

A husky, troubled voice came out of the crowd. It was Ganga, sweaty, pushing himself between the people, out of breath, his shirt opened at the chest.

The people surrounded Kimbo and one by one they came up and touched his arm, looking at his weary, watery eyes. The bison-man Ganga came up. His head was bowed, his mighty shoulders hunched. When he confronted the ashen, beaten figure before him, he could not raise his head. They never spoke in that long moment, and when Ganga walked past his two companions followed, seizing the hands of the tall, black man, touching his scorched ashen shoulders. His eyes shone with a faraway look, a strange candour of peace and frailty.

Bascombe, the Brave

Bascombe had fished all night. Soaked and worn out, he crouched over his little pirogue to escape the wrath of the storm snarling from the east behind roaring waves that tossed him high to the black clouds, which only a moment ago had hovered harmlessly over him. Pinning the oars under his feet, he grasped the sides of the boat for support.

Already his whole catch and the water bottle had been thrown out of the boat in the frantic upheavals. But the calabash was still tied to his toes. Only yesterday, he stood on shore and once more chastised Bolai, Bunsee and even Pa Hernandez, and the rest of them for going into his secret fishing grounds.

He laughed at them for being cowards, scorned their small catch and curled his fingers before their eyes in threatening gestures. For he was Bascombe the Brave, having no fear for man or the ocean.

"Bet you doh go out tomorrow. Is full moon, and crab running. Water rough like hell." Bolai sneered at him.

"You talking bull! And who you talking to?" Bascombe shouted as he pointed into Bolai's face.

"Man does be bad on land not in the sea," Bunsee answered quietly as he scraped the barnacles off his pirogue.

"Put you money where you mouth is and see ah doh do it. You feel you talking to a booboo? Look, I grow up in sea water. The sea is me godfather. You know dat! I ent fraid sea and I ent fraid fish," Bascombe bellowed.

"You going to meet you match one day, Bad John," Bolai said.

"Look, you threatening me or what? Bet ah buss a lash on you head for talking chupidness," Bascombe retorted.

"Ai, all you keep quiet, man. Too much noise!"

The voice came from the bent old man coming from behind the row of pirogues. His hair was loose and grey, his sapodilla-brown skin wrinkled.

Bascombe turned to the old man who approached them. "Look, Pa. Tell you boys keep quiet."

"He betting he going out tomorrow," Bunsee said to the old man.

"Going out! Let him do it. Not safe. Look, watch the sky and feel the wind."

"Watch it, ahready. Pa, you ent going to stop me if ah want to go. As long as I have these oars, I ent fraid nothing."

Bascombe turned to Pa Hernandez, scowling at the stooped figure who propped himself against the open boat, looking towards the sea.

Turning to Bunsee he shouted, "What you betting?"

"My whole box ah hooks and dat net over there. Cost me three hundred dollars," Bunsee answered.

"Doh be foolish, son," Pa Hernandez said.

But Bascombe had already collared Bolai and was shaking him, "Look, doh run eh, two ah all you. I coming back before morning right here!"

So late that night, he went out alone as he was accustomed to – the smoky oil-lantern swayed above his head as he leant on the oars. The muscles rippled beneath his cool black skin, his strong thighs angled against the small craft. A cold determined look was in his eyes. And from the bucket came the stench of herring bait.

Now beyond the shallows of the open sea, silvery in the moonlight, the leaden ripples lapped against the bow of his boat. On the banks, the small breakers charged with the incoming tide, foamed where the sand raised itself in smooth mounds.

He rowed steadily, past Dead Man's point, past Goodridge and the Pole, around the lighthouse, past those bands of undercurrent that moved in perilous convolutions swirling his craft against thrashing waves. The selfsame waves that swallowed up Rolly and Garcon and caused the whole village to go into mourning.

Now, white teeth glinting in the moonlight, he flexed his muscles and laughed at the storm with derisive scorn. Was he not Bascombe, the cunning, master of wave and tide, and the fisher who always dared depths unknown? Did he not always survive the fury of the storm and the bitter winds that tore under his skin as he paddled alone and unafraid, guided only by his expert knowledge of the clouds and the stars? Did he not always venture into thunder storms while others chose to remain at home cowering, mending their nets?

He thought of himself not only as the undisputed champion of the sea, but in his invulnerability, unconquerable. The thought enlivened his mind, enraptured his heart; and this night, it swelled his chest until pride, like some unseen force, caused a rush of blood to ripple through his massive arms clutching the sides of the boat.

A ghastly moon glowed feebly as he struggled. To avoid water pouring into his boat he threw his weight from side to side. He rocked and he fell, as the boat slid down the splashy walls of water. His head was thrown backwards as the small prow of his craft pointed to the heavens.

Riding down the side of a large wave, his boat leant to one side as he braced himself to counteract the tilt with the weight of his body. In an instant, he was conscious of the deep black chasm beneath him. Suddenly, he heard a crack, and he fell on the bottom of the boat; the seat had ruptured under the strain. With his legs thrown up, the oars and his bucket disappeared overboard but the calabash still clung to his toes. And for the first time he began to worry.

He worked the calabash like a madman, bailing out the water that swirled around his feet. But the storm continued unabated, as if in challenge to Bascombe's stubborn strength and courage.

A mountainous wave came like a black cloud poised low and grim over the water. It rose like some haunting apparition, its top a crowning, foaming crest, that glistened in the moonlight and Bascombe was engulfed, caught in the midst of the monstrous bank of water that nearly filled his boat. Once more he continued furiously, like a devil possessed, to stop the ocean from sinking his craft. As he panicked, the grinning faces of Bolai and Bunsee flashed before him.

Tossed about, with the loss of his oars, the terror of the night descended upon him; the cold dread of despair and loneliness. Lips parted as if in prayer, Bascombe looked up to the moon, as he wheeled around in his battered boat, pummelled and tossed like a toy in the rumbling, frothing ocean. He became despondent. He wept. The truth came to him like whiplash, louder in his mind than the peal of thunder that seemed to seal his fate. Now he remembered Pa Hernandez's words of warning.

Round and round he spun in his broken tub, eddying over the treacherous waters. The tossing had weakened him until, lying at the bottom of the boat spent and broken, he felt himself thrown out by some invisible force. The coil of rope fastened to the stern tightened around his waist as the little boat snapped in two. He felt himself falling, the rush of waters swallowed up his body.

Blackness. He grasped desperately, his hands outstretched, clawed, beat frantically. He tried to remain afloat but each time he raised his head, a towering mass of water crashed over him.

Only a moment ago he had seen the vision of a mighty spirit, a destructive force riding behind the great wave; he felt it in the power of the winds; heard it in the bellow of thunder; saw it in the sharp tongues of lightning flashes. Overpowering. In the pallid glow of the silent moon, the only witness to his perilous ordeal.

Now he felt the tremor of his heart and the intense pain running from his lungs along his spine, upwards to his brain, exploding in his ear drums. His body stiffened, convulsed as he plunged down into nothingness.

The next morning, a soothing calm transformed the surface of the ocean and with the winds waning the swells lifted gently. Clouds wafted across the azure immensity of the sky and the horizon shimmered in the distant grey haze. Bunsee went to Pa Hernandez to collect his box of hooks and his net.

So they found Bascombe washed ashore cold and stiff, five miles away from the bay where he was accustomed to stand knee-deep in the water alongside his pirogue laden with his great catch, rolling his eyes, boastingly beating his chest.

Trotters

Bent like her walking stick, Ma Abdool lived a frugal life, balancing her budget like the basket atop her head that floated precariously with straggly bundles of yellowing chive and pale ochroes which like her dry self had long passed the age of slime. Yet she planted, the only way she knew of, for a small income so meagre at times that, after Choy Wing closed his shop, she would blow out her flambeau, knot the coins with her orhini, raise her eyes to the dark heavens as if in supplication, and walk the tired road home.

Zobida, her new daughter-in-law, bright eyed but plump and smooth like 'bigan', lived with her. She cooked and kept house, collected coconut husks and, whenever the wind littered the yard, bent with one arm behind her back, the other rotating in rapid arcs with her cocoyea broom, heaping up the trash that went up later in dry leaf smoke.

Late one afternoon, Ma Abdool returned from selling.

"You na cookam yet, gul. And night done come."

"Mai, ah done put the water to boil."

"Wata... wata... what you make am?"

"Mai, Azard say he goh take some soup tonight."

"Soop... soop. We is creoni? Only creoni does drinkam soup."

"But Ma, it still have piece a sada roti."

"Bete, I wantam choka, too. See you have am damadol and chonkay it."

Azard worked in the sugar estate. When he married Zobida, two of his best friends boycotted the wedding. They listened to the rumour that Zobida was 'dougla', even though the bride's parents denied it. Later, many times sitting on the doorstep, as he rummaged her head on his lap, he would stop for long moments, his fingers probing the strands of hair behind her ear, and watch their natural curl as he thought of black pepper grains. He wondered what brand of lice fed on 'dougla' heads, but musingly smiled for he had loved Zobida and that was what counted.

She was so different from other Muslim girls. He liked the way she carried the pitch oil pan of water on her head, her thick calves bouncing along the railway road like cork balls, her splayed toes stubby like a morocoy's. But most of all, it was her waist – rounded and moulded – rotating in that flawless rhythm as she walked, dizzying his head until his heart was seized by joyous palpitations.

Azard knew of the mild bickerings at home. That clash between the old world philosophy and the challenging horizons of anticipated resistance. The strong-willed hard-core precepts clashing against the liberal exuberance of new world ethics. Yet he loved them both: the caring mother and the loving wife.

He sweetened their lives with brown sugar, cane syrup, and at times molasses he brought home in his food carrier, and had more than once intoxicated them with puncheon rum spirited away from the sugar estate distillery in his bamboo walking stick. He was a panboiler assistant. He would pass the gateman after work, head aloft, walking briskly, the small parcels of brown sugar concealed, tied around his calves under his baggy pants.

"Gul, I don't know how we goh make out nah; Ma doh

eat this and you doh like dat. This kinda thing could drive a man crazy. Just now we goh have two pots in this house, one for you and one for she."

"You think is dry baggee I go eat every day, Azard. You, yuh self. I want solid food. I doh want anybody to call me like Ma, mangy Madinga," Zobida replied.

"I know, I could see for myself but you know how them old people accustom to they own diet," Azard said.

"Since I small, I know baggee bound to be on the table. But I used to like Johnny bake. Ma used to cook roti, but I always used to ask her to make a fat one for me. And was chocolate tea with fry fish and salt beef," Zobida answered.

"So, is true you have a liking for creole food?" Azard asked.

"Why not, and that is good food, too? Food without grease is like grass for cow."

Azard's suspicion of Zobida's blood strain continued to grow. Not only because of the physical attributes of her buxom body, but also her flair for cooking exotic, greasy dishes.

Tonight it was soup time. Ma Abdool leant her stick in a corner and gently placed her basket of unsold provisions on the floor. She took an enamel cup of water and gargled, spitting expertly out into the yard. Azard brought her roti on a plate and she sat alone near the doorway.

"Try some soup Ma, the choka ent hot yet," Zobida said.

Zobida stirred the iron pot. The smells of boiling plantain and yams that came back from the market and long dumplings she had kneaded out of flour and cornmeal were strong. For added taste she had included coconut milk, pigeon peas and, secretly, her own concoction.

Azard took his simmering bowl and sat at the table;

Zobida's share was the largest. They ate under the kerosene lamp, cooling the food by blowing on the hot viscous pottage.

Ma Abdool sipped, watching in the dim light the bluish tinge of molten eddoes floating in her colourful enamel bowl. She sat, as always, on the floor, hunched up like a relic, the curve of her bony chest depleted, her bowl of soup on a bench.

The flickering kerosene lamp threw large shadows on the walls. Azard's silhouette assumed a giant torso, Zobida's a shapeless heap. At the family meal only the smattering of lips broke the silence. The soup went down well, Zobida went back to the pot and poured out generously again, taking time to share with her husband.

Ma Abdool enjoyed her portion; the dumplings were lumpy but tasty. She went through them with stubborn gums and munched, relishing the taste.

Then suddenly she held her jaw and called out in pain.

"O Gard, stone, Beta." Ma Abdool held her face with both hands, rose towards the doorway, but changed her course and came back to the table.

"Mai, what wrong?" Zobida asked.

Azard looked at his mother, putting down his own spoon. A chunk of cassava filled out his cheeks.

Ma Abdool held something in Her hands which she brought towards the lamplight and then threw them on the table. They rolled across the table like dice and Zobida pushed a plate to cover them. But Azard, observing her quick movements, gently pushed her plate aside and picked up the bits of bone and brought them nearer to the lampshade, examining them as Zobida held her breath.

"What that, Beta?" Ma Abdool asked innocently.

Azard scrutinised the pieces of bone in the palm of his hand.

He placed them in Zobida's hand and looked at her long and hard.

Ma Abdool looked into her son's eyes then shifted her gaze to Zobida's face. Mother and son awaited an answer.

"Is meat bone," Zobida said at last.

Azard, wanting to confirm the discovery further, kept staring at her.

"What kind?" he insisted.

"Trotters," she answered.

"Trotters. What is dat?" Azard asked.

"I hear people by the market does call it so."

"Trotters, what you mean by trotters? You does buy from that Potogee man? That you put in the food?" Azard asked.

Ma Abdool continued looking at them. Her heart skipped a beat. A smile escaped Azard's face, his eyelashes rose surreptiously.

"What that, Beta?" she enquired tremblingly.

"Nothing. Is beef bone. Let me see if they have more." He assured her, turning to stir her soup, laughter choking in his throat. Ma Abdool felt relief.

"Chotters is beef bone, Beta?" Ma Abdool still asked the inevitable question.

Azard never answered his mother. He turned away from her, gave out a throttled, piggy grunt and sought refuge from his mother across the table. But Zobida was looking intently at her own soup, her lips churned, making slurping noises, hiding a smile.

Azard thought about the rumour that kept his friends away from his wedding and he became more convinced than ever that the rumour might be true.

'To hell with them,' he thought to himself, again almost blurting out aloud. He loved Zobida and that was that. After all, she was his wife and if she wanted to eat pig foot at times, why not? That was her own business. And who cared whether she was Dougla, part Creoni or even a full bloodied Creole. Azard probed into the murky depths of his own bowl. Pushing eddoes, cush-cush and dumplings aside, he searched until he found a knuckle, lifted it into the chasm of his mouth, gnawed into gristle and bone and, savouring the crumbled morsel, turned and winked at his wife.

As for Ma Abdool, she resumed her position at the doorway and abandoned her plate and roti on her bench. She stooped over her bowl, smattered her lips and called out to Zobida.

"Beti, yuh haveam any more chotters?"

Caesar

I had known him for only three years but it could have been thirty. Mark Lancelot Robles, impetuous, adventurous and young, from London where he had schooled and learned to fly, taking on a job with the local airlines. His parents died early and his only sister had long married in the Far East, he told me.

I had not seen him for months, then one night he rapped on my door. He stood on the porch, wet hair streaming over his eyes, the pullover zipped to his throat, travelling bag in hand and Caesar, the Mynah bird, proud and blue-black, perched on his arm, scarcely discernible in the darkness.

"Sorry to make it so late, chum, but Eastern only flies out at one-thirty on week days," he said, wrapped in the shadows of greenhorn ferns under the awning.

"Have to go, man. Another job, maybe – another life. You know how it is? One place, one type of work can tire you at times, and one always wants to move around." His voice trailed off.

"But Christ, where are you going at this hour? What's going on, man? Haven't seen you in years."

Ignoring my questions, he came closer, the blunt tips of his brogues visible under the gaberdine trousers draping his legs. I saw a weary face with a far away look and eyes with their scurry of lines furrowing to newer depths.

"Look, I brought you Caesar. Know you will look after him – dog chow will do for him."

He lowered his arms and the bird, shining black, leapt on the balustrade, the deep guttural croaks coming out of its tight throat, the wattles flapping behind its head.

"But where's Margot?"

He ignored the question; he did not look up. His right hand kept patting the bird. He seemed worried. Then he smiled and looked over my head, as if he had forgotten something and was trying to remember it. Caesar inched along the balustrade, its piercing cries loud in the darkness.

"So long, pal. Will write you about it – it's a long story. Going to California – new job."

He withdrew into the shadows and was gone, leaving in his wake the trail of camphor and perfume. On the balustrade Caesar emitted a high-pitched note, piercingly loud, as if it suspected that I knew the whole story.

The first time we met was at the Airlines' party. He enjoyed the music, intoxicated by Choy's bongos. Hands full, a girl on each arm, he jumped, pranced, scuttled across the floor, eyes sparkling with joy. When he came near, I saw that infectious smile. He poured a drink into my glass and we toasted as if we were old acquaintances celebrating some occasion. And it did have a special meaning, for it was the beginning of a long and lasting friendship.

He was living in an apartment high up the valley among the houses that were spread out on larger plots overlooking the city. Between flights he found time for his nursery of beautiful orchids. He had a beaten-up old guitar on which he picked the long-forgotten country ballads of England. But it was with Caesar, his pet bird, that he really spent most of his time, teaching it to talk.

On its perch, Caesar stood, a velvety sheen of black – indigo stretched taut over its agile body. Eyes, double spots of burning coals rimmed in yellow, were sharp like the yellow beak ending in a scriber point. Quickly the flat myoclonic head would jerk from side to side, restless as if to heed the call of the wild or a lurking danger that could mean the difference between life or death. Now a melodic croak would escape its red-tongued mouth, then a hissing, high-pitched screech as it hopped closer to the water jar. Stretching his hand, Mark would take it up on his shoulder where it whistled and talked, pecking at his earlobes playfully. Passing him on to me, he would say, "Take him, Willi," and to the bird, "Whistle, Caesar. Say something." Mark would whisper in its ear and the Mynah would roll out its loud notes, strutting, making quick turning movements, pivoting on its feet.

We spent time playing rummy or tennis, or on other evenings we walked the savannah gardens where Caesar delighted in its short flights among the shady trees. Caesar flew from shoulder to shoulder, flapping its jet black wings in glee, mimicking the honking horns of passing traffic. Mark always patted its head while he blew his breath over it. We never bothered about the curious glances or the remarks that were thrown at us about big men playing with a black bird. For us, Caesar remained a link in our friendship; that was until Margot came.

There was that ease about her fluid movement that was captivating in the careless toss of her hair. Propped by her arms on the grassy lawn that afternoon, she turned to face us as we passed. Her little dachshund posed a noisy nuisance, and Caesar mimicked the barking dog.

The yellow leaves fell gently from black branches as the chill of the April winds careened across the hollows, and bits of popsicle wraps and cigarette stubs spiralled up with the dust. The slight drizzle came at an appropriate time and precipitated the meeting when, grabbing her skirt against her pink thighs, she nearly ran into us from behind the huge rock. She laughed loudly, stumbling, as Mark grabbed her around her waist. The weeks that followed saw us making more visits to the gardens. We became a common though odd sight – two men with a black bird perched on their shoulders and a woman with a short sausage-like dog, walking over the grass.

"Can I take him on my arm, Mark?" She would ask, putting out her manicured fingers as Caesar hopped on to her bangled arm, pecking at the coloured beads. She was fascinated with Caesar's sheen of jet-black feathers, its red feet, and the agility with which the bird picked up the food, gobbling it down.

The wedding took place seven months afterwards. A dry, sunless afternoon with the flutter of lemon organza and matching scarves, sequined to sparkle like the bright eyes of young prospective brides, who traipsed over the lawn. And Margot's dreamy look pervaded the ceremony, as she stood radiant, happy, surrounded by friendly glances and pleasantries. Somehow, Mark looked nervous. But head coiffured and held beneath the primrose net, Margot remained doubtless, half-concealed behind the gauzy veil.

With my job transfer, my visits became less frequent, but whenever I turned up at their home, the afternoons were memorable. We played cards, talked and, over lemonade, spent the time looking down at the lighted city or at the cool, sheltered landscape of mountain ranges. In the beginning, Margot loved her new home and the high, airy surroundings and, with Mark, pottered around the living room, decorating it with macrame and ceramics. There was that thick brown rug he had brought from Mexico, all aflame in red and orange rays of sunset over a head motif which was the central theme of the decor. Beneath this stood her lean, glassy cabinet, with a display of crystals, mugs which Mark had collected as souvenirs along his flights; brass vessels from the East, leather craft from Brazil and Paraguay, dolls from Dominica.

Holding up the little primitive oil painting from Haiti, she asked, "Is it right here, darling? It's just the right size too."

"Suit yourself. Lower, maybe, an inch." Mark looked up touching her cheeks with his hands.

"You know, Mark, I can see myself sitting right on the porch looking up to the sky, just when you are on that DC7."

"Heavenly, isn't it?" Mark replied, the flash of his teeth white behind the curtain.

"Breathe in the air, honey. It's paradise. Look, there's the highway – all those sodium lights."

"Doesn't it remind you of the runway?"

"You are smart." Mark whispered into her ear as he stood behind her, his strong arms over her shoulders embracing her neck.

Below them, the valley dropped in tiers of lush green foliage dotted along the surrounding slopes with golden patches of pouis and flaming flambouyant. To the left stood the silent grey cliffs, with the hard rock faces poised over the valleys, over which the morning mists drifted in blankets of feathery puffs. Margot relished the scenic beauty and for this Mark delighted in the choice of his home. Although placed high up on this plateau, perched ideally over the romantic landscape of the city, the sea, and the cascading valleys of dense, cool vegetation, their home did not fulfil Margot's happiness entirely.

With Mark away on his flights, on long afternoons, she would sit on the porch on the same rattan rocker which creaked each time she leant over the railing, to catch a glimpse of the falling landscape beneath her. In her mind the loneliness dragged on like some ache. The longing she had for Mark, probably enclosed now within the aluminium cockpit over the distant seas, brought her agony closer to a frightening belief. A belief that the pain would soon evolve itself into an unbearable pang of despair. Not far below, the light of the Jacksons' kitchen was bright over the gas ranges where the aproned, chubby figure of a mother held a saucepan over the heads of the four children seated around the table at supper. Margot felt herself shudder at the responsibility of raising a family. The idea tormented her, terrified her, and looking down at the little family over supper with Mrs Jacksons' abdomen already distended with the fifth unborn, Margot felt the sharpening sense of terror increasing to high pitch in her mind.

She jumped at the shrill cry of Caesar, coming from the back porch. The bird had remained so quiet during the last hour, scarcely chirping as though allowing her to meditate on her own loneliness. Fireflies emerged out of the night forest. The frogs began to croak from beneath the spreading chataigne. The bats made whirring sounds as they knifed through the air overhead. Margot stood up and turned into the sitting room, closing the door of the front porch, shutting off the panoramic vista of lights and sounds.

Even with all the good things of life, a comfortable home and a happy marriage, Margot had become gradually despondent. After she watered the plants in the morning she turned to Caesar for company. Then the walks came, afternoon walks, strolls along the winding road downhill, bringing some small relief from her boredom.

She passed the Jacksons', the Titus', the Hamiltons' and the Masons', and the wide flower gardens with the collections of orchids. She passed the playground where the little boys played football. Reaching the corner she came up to the mansion with the alabaster pillars entwined with vines from the orchard of pomegranate and figs. This was the Ramos' house, set back behind the cluster of bougainvillea and marigolds and the pendulous baskets of ferns. A brown dog, as short-legged as hers, long ears hanging, came out in a rush. It ran up to the gate, barking at her own dachshund. The dog pressed at the wiremesh, sniffing and barking, while her own dog pulled, straining on the leash to meet the other.

"Wants to be friends, I see," Mr Ramos' voice was foreign. She replied almost instantly.

"Yes, the same breed, I suppose. Only yours seems to be all brown. A good stock, she's come from good parentage. Papers could show it, had three litters; all successful."

"Have you been living up there long?" Mr Ramos asked, gazing into her face, his shoulders hunched over his cup of tea, the eyes penetrating, so unlike Mark's, his dark hair so different from Mark's.

"A little over six months," she replied.

"Yes, I know. You are Mrs Robles...the pilot, he is the

chap from England, of course."

"The garden is so lovely," she spoke quietly, sipping the tea, and her voice brought him out of his thoughts.

He looked at her, when he heard her voice. "Grandfather built it, but we keep it well", he said. Then, in a lighter tone of voice, "Want to exchange places? Your view is grand. I know the house. Used to belong to the Simpsons. He was a friend of the family before he died. He was from England, too. Came over quite young. Used to work with one of those oil merchants downtown, Henderson I think it was. Shipping, you know, commerce, that sort of thing."

"Are you serious?"

"About what?"

"About exchanging places." They laughed. They both laughed. And the conversation, friendly but almost meaningless, went on into the afternoon and into other afternoons whenever Margot dropped in for tea.

As she returned home Caesar's piercing shriek came through the front door. Loud and shrill.

"Evening, Caesar. Poor thing must be hungry." She bent over the Mynah's head and touched the loose wattle behind its head. She stretched her hand beneath Caesar and he jumped on her wrist, pecking at her watch with its red beak. Caesar preened itself between mouthfuls of chow emitting a whistle now and again. Margot lifted it up blowing her breath over its sleek head.

Over the months Caesar had grown to know Margot and would stand perched on her fingers whistling, talking, reaching out its neck to the bangles around her wrist. In Caesar she saw Mark, so completely Mark in all the sounds it made. She felt the closeness, his closeness as he would stand behind her, hugging her around her arms with that strong intimate hold. He would whisper as he threw his air bag on the floor, "How is Caesar today?" Then unwrapping the little gift, the trinket he brought for her, he would open the other package of Mynah food he had brought along. It would always be the same, standing in his pilot uniform, white and blue, the brass buttons shining against his coat, the engraved wings on his chest. He came up the steps, cap in hand, the blond head rising over the wall, opening his arms to greet her.

"Mark, I am dying to go to the beach one day!" she said.

"Look, you have the whole mountain range for yourself and all of nature."

"True, darling, but nature must be enjoyed outdoors," she laughed.

One day midweek, when, according to the programme he had tacked on to the wall in the bedroom he should have been in Mexico, Mark found himself with a break in schedule. He decided to come home and spend the two days before beginning the next roster with his wife. He arrived late at night and decided to surprise her. He came up the steps noiselessly. He pushed the door of the porch and tiptoed in the gallery. The leather couch was in the corner and the small table with the magazines and journals to the left. He placed the bag on the floor before the door and felt for the key in his coat. There it was beneath the parcel, the gift he had brought her, this gift he had asked the girl at the duty-free counter to wrap with the shiny ribbon. The smooth paper felt soft to his touch. It reminded him of Margot. What would she say now, in her surprise? He could imagine the surprise in her big brown eyes, tossing her hair over her shoulders, the nightie around her soft body. Maybe she would scream out with pleasure. She always greeted him with passionate kisses; they were still lovers.

Then his eyes caught the glint on the table like a pair of eyes in the darkness couch. He stooped over, holding the key in his hand; it came from two drinking glasses. At first he thought of the Burgundy he had brought from New York, from the little wine shop with the bottles all suspended from the ceiling, some encased in baskets from Italy. Margot liked Italian wines. With the key in his hand he turned to the door but he stopped, hesitating, looking around. Those glints, those drinking glasses. He stood motionless, wearing his silence like an invisible coat. Two glasses. He turned and picked one up. His guess was right, the strong alcoholic smell was there, in the small pool of liquid still at the bottom. He picked up the other gently; there was more liquid in it, a crimson stain at the edge. It was then he heard the giggle, the laugh; it came like a shot in the night through the burglar-proof fretwork from the bedroom. He stood frozen, shocked, and the heartbeats rose from his chest in wild thumps, he imagined, echoing across the living room.

Instinctively he retreated, putting the glasses gently on the table, bending his head low behind the door. He peered through the burglar-proof fretwork, the curtains behind were hanging loosely. The little dachshund was coiled asleep on the rug near the wall. He heard the low ticks of the clock. He scanned the room, his ears cocked. Then the laughter came again. He jumped as if emerging from some frightening dream – the realisation, the sudden impact hit him like a rock hurled from the darkness of his own room. He clutched the bag – reeled against the wall. He never knew how long he stood with his back against the wall, confused, shattered, gripped by the sound of that laughter, the second laughter, male, rising above Margot's own. He did not remember descending the steps into the yard and going out along the road, where he drifted aimlessly. His eyes were glued to the porch, to the front door. Had he stepped into the wrong home?

He waited in the darkness behind the clumps of bush below the mango tree. Twice he felt for his cigarettes, but decided against it. The mosquitoes hummed around his face. From there, the front porch of his house was still visible, the roof outlined vaguely against the night sky. He waited patiently, the bag at his feet, right hand in his coat pocket twirling the key to his front door. Who was it? How long had it been going on? Was he an old friend?

He stared. He stared into darkness, recalling the memorable events in his life with her, when he first met her, in the savannah – with Caesar. The wedding came to his mind vividly. His friends were all there, some on the lawn sipping champagne offering toasts. Who was it? It might be one of his friends, one of his guests. Or someone she had known long before he had met her. He kept looking at the porch and waited. Mark could not tell whether the figure walking down the road had come out of his front porch. His thoughts were broken – the discovery was too startling, numbing his senses. The violation terrified him yet he did not panic. The discipline came from his training as a pilot. He was only conscious of his heartbeats, the lump that rose in his throat. He leant against the tree and dozed. Out of nowhere a man came down the road, his face lit up by a cigarette. Mark felt the lump in his throat getting bigger. He trembled with apprehension.

Mark came out of the undergrowth, leaving his bag below the tree, and followed the figure some distance ahead of him. It was a man he had never seen before. Mark's eyes stuck onto the back of the figure receding in the darkness, his shirt barely visible each time he passed before the dimly lit galleries of the houses along the road.

Keeping at a steady stride, Mark reached the corner house, where the road junction broadened. The man was nowhere; he had disappeared. Mark stood behind the lamp post, where only a moment ago the figure had been illuminated beneath the pale glow. He looked to the right, then to the left where the dead end came abruptly in the heap of rotting car bodies. Mark turned away, puzzled, but something caught his eye. It was a light in the corner house. It was not there when he approached the corner only a moment ago. He looked across at the great house, into the room where the light had just appeared. He was almost sure and yet he could not relate the putting on of the light with the man he had just followed. Mark hesitated and seeing no further activity in the big house, walked slowly up the road.

At eight o'clock the next morning Mark came up his front steps. He pushed the porch door aside. The glasses were no longer there, only the water-rings, the stains were on the arm rests of the couch. The swelling returned to his throat. He knocked. He waited. He knocked louder, rapping the glass pane, peeping through the burglar-proof. He called – the same cheerful voice.

"Margot, it's me..." He heard the bed spring noises, the shuffling sounds and the bedroom door opened. Margot came out, the sleep still in her eyes which lit up in surprise. She clutched the nightie around her throat.

"Change of flight, darling?" she asked, a little curious, a little perturbed. Instinctively she threw her arms over his shoulders, pushing up her cheeks, pouting her mouth to be kissed.

"Never thought you would get a change of flight in the middle of the week dear." She swayed, her voice crackled, somewhat dismayed by the gentle peck Mark put on her upturned lips. She was disappointed at the slight brush of his lips; the lifeless, passionless peck. But his eyes had the same blue sparkle. He turned to put his bag down and surprisingly gave her shoulders a tight hug, an act that came like an act of assurance. She followed him into the kitchen.

"Must be hungry, darling. But I never thought you would come in this early. Some change in the schedule?" she asked again.

"Changes come along unexpectedly," he answered passing her at the stove where she had the saucepan already sizzling.

He came out in his slippers and walked across to the back porch where he found Caesar. He held out his hand and the bird whistled. It pecked at Mark's palm where the brown pellets were fresh out of the pack. Mark took the bird outside. Margot looked on. A quietness came over her. For the first time since her marriage, she felt distanced from her husband. She stirred the saucepan, mechanically, absentmindedly, her mind occupied by the events of the night before. Mark had gone through the door with Caesar, not even saying anything to her.

Margot laid out the table, two eggs, sunny-side up,

sprinkled with fine black pepper, slices of lemon at the side of the saucer and buttered toast. She filled his cup with his favourite Blue Mountain coffee, hot out of the percolator. She placed the napkins with the silver and took the glass of juice out of the refrigerator. She wiped her hands and looked through the window. Mark was not there. She came down the steps. "Mark!" she called. The steps descended over the washroom and the garage. Mark was not in the garden. She was puzzled and distressed.

Retracing her steps into the kitchen, she felt abandoned. She put a saucer over the cup of coffee and placed a gauze cover over the whole meal. She drank a glass of water from the refrigerator. It cooled her nerves. She regained her composure, at least temporarily. But the feeling of remorse grew until she found it difficult to remain calm. Morose, she lay on the couch thinking, absorbed by her guilt. She did not hear Mark return, never heard his footsteps. It was Caesar's loud croak that made her sit up suddenly. "Mark," she called instinctively. She looked into the kitchen, into the area around the porch at the rear of the building. To her surprise, Caesar was now on his perch. She hurried to the landing just in time to see him at the foot of the stairs. His back was towards her.

"Aren't you having breakfast, honey?"

"Not at all hungry," he replied. He kept on walking away from her.

"Are you going out again?" she asked a little louder.

But he was away, too far away to hear her; he did not reply. She came down three treaders of steps. Mark had gone through the garden gate and was out in the road.

"Gone for a walk alone?" Tense now, her fluttering eye

lids did not hide her feelings. She wondered.

The realisation hovered over her head before crashing down like a gong of truth. Had he suspected? It was impossible. The events were too far apart. Did someone in the district see? Mark knew no one, hardly ever spoke to anyone in the district. He was always flying, away from home. She went on to the porch and looked out. The landscape was bright, the sky a light blue. At first the low wall hid the whole view, but gradually the tree tops appeared as she walked slowly towards the rattan rocker. Mark's head appeared a dot, the sleeveless merino a white daub against the trees; the road, a ribbon at his feet. Where was he going, dressed like this? Unlike him. She turned towards the doorway and entered the room. It was then she saw the water-ring stains on the arm-rest of the couch. She paused, her heart raced.

When Mark returned, he entered the drawing room and took off his slippers. Margot came out of the kitchen and said. "Breakfast is getting cold, darling. Where did you go, Mark?

"Ah, just a little walk," he replied calmly.

He did not look up, but picked up his slippers and went into the bedroom. She heard the slippers fall on the floor. There was silence. Then she heard the shower, the falling water splashing against the bathroom door, which always remained open before – closed now as if to shut her off from his presence, out of his life. She bit her lips, looked through the bedroom over the bed, to the dressing table with all her lotions and perfumes, and felt trapped, suddenly a stranger in her own home.

When Mark came out of the shower, Margot was sitting in the gallery. She waited for him, knowing that he would change into his short cotton pants, as he was so accustommed to doing in the afternoons. Below her the tree tops shimmered, moved by a gentle breeze that rustled through the huge sapodilla tree growing next to the porch. She was unaware of the beauty in the rich greenery of cliffs that sparkled in the distance. She heard his footsteps. She turned to meet him but he was dressed in his pilots' uniform and in his boots, the bag in his hand. She was surprised, she looked up at him. "Going back so early darling? Thought you were on your two days."

"No, maybe next week. Flight schedules are chaotic now. Never know where I stand," he replied casually, too quietly.

He bent and kissed her, first on her cheek, then on her lips, but without the wild passion he always had for her.

"Take care. I will be back maybe by the weekend, if things work out."

"But aren't you going to eat something before you go, Mark?"

"It's O.K. I'm not really hungry."

She now felt disturbed, unwanted. He broke from her embrace and left through the door and quickly down the steps. The car had the airline emblem of wings and stars painted over the hood. Standing in the porch, she saw his head disappear. The door closed and there was a slight whiff of blue smoke at the rear as he drove off. She watched the car drive down the hill, moving slowly to avoid the small ruts. His departure happened so quickly. He never gave her the slightest indication that he was leaving, so unlike him, so abrupt. It was the first time he had left the very day he had come and he hadn't even mentioned that he would have to go. But it was his attitude, the cold change, that puzzled her. The silence. Then it dawned on her, as she stood on the porch, too preoccupied with her own thoughts, that he did not wave.

One week passed and Mark did not come home. She sat on the gallery pining, engulfed by her own melancholy solitude. The afternoon strolls to the Ramos' mansion were something of the past. Only Caesar's wild chirps and calls kept her from going out of her mind. The second week arrived, Monday then Tuesday, without any hope of his appearance. Thursday then Friday and the weekend came like an agony. She grew more nervous, her spirits shattered. A sense of isolation. Emptiness. At last he arrived. But with a bundle of books; it was peculiar. After greeting her, he immediately sat at the dining table and opened his books. He had to study, examinations were coming up. He needed the peace and the silence. She could not disturb him. He assured her that it would be a difficult examination and that pilots were to be selected for promotion based on the results. He studied long into the night. She became restless, despondent; he had grown calm, cold, detached, even from eating the meals she prepared.

The weeks followed in an atmosphere of gloom, his vacation weeks. He sat for hours with Caesar. Then he would take the bird into the garden, putting it down to walk along the gallery wall. Margot gradually felt more shut out by the indifference which grew daily, creating a wall between them. Finally it was complete silence. The serene antagonism was calculated. He barely uttered a word, face deep down over his books. He ate little: simple sandwiches, liver paste or marmalade over toast, and coffee. He drank it unsweetened now, as if to drown his own anguish by the amount he consumed.

One day he brought home a neatly wrapped parcel. She glanced through the bedroom curtain. He was unwrapping it on the bed, snapping the strings with a twist of his fingers, the stiff brown paper rustled. It was his shirts and a pair of trousers. A tag with the Chinese writing was pinned on to the garments.

She retreated, walking backwards, nearly tripping over the pouf and the centre table. In the gallery, she put down the duster and sat on the chair. Now dazed, the fact that Mark was having his clothes washed in the Chinese laundry downtown came as another shock, confirming her suspicion, which had been hovering like a cloud over her head. The helplessness drained her of strength. She was tormented by the bland look on his face. Recovering from her thoughts, she stood up.

The road uncoiled like a huge snake, the shallow ruts blotched like patches of scales. The short brown grass crept up at the sides like the slime in its path as it glided downhill between the row of houses with the wrought iron gates, wiremesh fences enclosing the gardens past the Jacksons' and the Titus', and the corner house with those huge ferns in identical shaped baskets under which she spent many afternoons having tea.

Her heart skipped a beat. The haunting eyes and dark groomed head appeared over the teacup with the thin veil of rising steam. The blue tiles on the floor, the Degas prints and the ferns all around her so cool and green. Then she heard the words again coming out of her mouth: "Cannot see you again. Never. You must understand... please, and don't try to see me." Distorted in the wind, the words came out haltingly as she pleaded. Then gathering up her skirt, tossing the brown hair over her shoulders, she dashed out of the porch, downstairs into the driveway, along the paved yard to the gate. Her face drained of its colour – her lips quivered, a frantic look in her eyes. She ran up the road...leaving the gate opened. She nearly ran into a couple walking towards her. That happened some time ago, when Mark had gone on his new work shift.

Two weeks later, after Mark's appearance like a ghost before my front door with Caesar that night, I had another call. This time it was also late in the evening. I had just taken Caesar inside and covered the cage. The man standing on the porch before the front door was of medium height with dark, well-groomed hair. His eyes were warm and friendly and the skin across his cheeks was white and taut.

"Are you Mr Chen?"

"Yes."

"Margot asked me to get in touch with you."

"Where is she?" I asked, surprised both by the appearance of the stranger and the message he brought.

"In the hospital. Just moved her there."

"Is she sick?"

"No," he said almost in a whisper. "She's dead." I was stunned. I looked at him closely.

"How did it happen?" I asked, shocked at the news, looking into his face for an answer.

"Man in the trailer said she must have seen him. It was impossible that she couldn't, that she didn't... ...Said she seemed lost, wild. She just stepped into the road ...right in front of the truck and turned to face him, the truck."

I was thinking of Mark. "How did you know where to

find me?" I asked.

"She told me about you. She left a note with me." The man opened his hand and handed me the piece of crumpled paper. On it was my address with the message, scrawled by her hand in pencil, "Hope you will let Mark know that it was all a mistake. I love him. Tell him that." And suddenly, from the rear, out of the cloth-covered cage, Caesar emitted its high-pitched shriek as if it had understood.

The Killing of Sanchez

In one movement he raised his arm, heavily bangled, taut against the sleeveless leathercoat, and the blade sank into the balata tree – vibrating with that metallic clang of cold steel. It was only his way of saying that he was Saragun, true warrior, chief of the whole tribe. Nephew of Mumtaz, that ferocious dougla with the longest dread locks, gun runner, contraband king, who, in the days of Kincaid, Mano and Ghost, had the record and boasted of it: of outwitting the coast guards with their fast boats equipped with spotlights and submachine guns; bringing in Carupano whisky, fat morocoys, bags of tobacco, spiky iguanas with their hind claws pinned into flesh behind their own tails, kegs of honey – the finest from all Spain – the cages of exotic birds, orioles, troupiales, parrots and bright-plumed macaws. Their cantankerous screechings often made the secret skirmishes more perilous in the mangrove recesses, because of marine police who patrolled the coastline under the dreaded commandant Mendoza.

He was the enemy of the Warahoons, his thirst for blood equalled only by his sadistic passion for torturing his captives in the narrow cells beneath the rat-infested dungeons that stank of rancid urine. Cells like those of Seville where the prisoners were chained to the walls of the courtyard and flogged till sunrise – the hour of benediction in the prison chapel. Those were the days, too, of Balbosa. Strongman, tyrant, black patch over his left eye, making him even more horrific in his aimless swagger. The haughty Lopez, strikingly tall, open-mouthed, the shock of red beard dangling like his scrotum past his knees, swearing after mouthfuls of wine, his hand forever hovering over the dagger at his waist.

They met at the appointed time of eleven p.m., the hour as sinister as the surroundings. A cocoa grove, silk-cotton shade, the gri-gri background with the night forest noises, not more than two kilometres from the deepest ravine at the roadside, far from the bulwark of road blocks attended by trigger-happy security men, perched low over their land cruisers black in the shadows, their woollen caps hooded their heads from the cold winds. In the forest gloom, before midnight, the group was complete with Manickchand and Jojo, robed in dashiki; Manuel too, with Tote, until they all stood with their Yamahas 1000 draped with heavy knapsacks strung low over the fuel tanks, and further into the dismal cove was the faint glimmer of other machines just as fast and in readiness.

There was Ganga with four hundred pounds of ganja; Manuel carried four hundred too. Rannie toted only two bags. Tallboy, one. Quiet in the reticent darkness was Ojo, his head plaited, matted locks, rust dry and held aloft by pins, his lips smirked, nervously and trembled as though from apprehension of danger. At his side was Bolo on the run from the law along with Sagan, who was blacker than tar, stunted stalwart, who made up for his loss in height and his slowness of speech by the spreading of his limbs and his strength. His hands were so large, they could husk a coconut with no fuss. Marquez slouched; he was of Spanish extract – deadly with his knife and always ready to claim his ancestry from Spain.

A despicable band of scoundrels, vagabonds, some swearing by the Holy Virgin Mary, others by Jah, an admixture of strong origins speaking in subdued tongues but gathered here for a common purpose: to decipher the coded message out of the tattooed sheet under the light of the egg yolk moon. Lawless cut-throats, rebels, rapists, plunderers. But above all... dope pushers with contacts in Peru and Venezuela and Columbia. Drug-runners who were renowned in the Virgin Islands – those strategically positioned bases for South American marijuana, so much in demand that packaging operations necessitated sophisticated machinery for weighing, labelling, shrink-wrapping and printing in an anonymous illegible flourish, on bright yellow cellophane, giving the semblance of butter and cheese coming out of hatchways of lighters somewhere on the Spanish coast act under the scrutiny of custom officials who seemed blind in their blue-coated ignorance, as the large pallets swung over their heads with the big labels imprinted in red "Fernleaf" over the stamped-apron-transfer of some Australian, dimpled maid.

Then the large caravans hitched in double trailers, behind the gleaming Macks, fuming mufflers overhead and sparkling mag rims, would move out in style onto the open highways. No one could have imagined this mode of transport would have been so open as they ignored the authorities, some of whom were long ago bribed by that notorious Almandoz who blasphemed, deprecating all the officials as useless and stupid and then boasted about it to Ramirez, that other clandestine mogul from El Tigre who defied everyone in the operations, setting down his own rules, enforcing them by the power of his wealth and the brutality of his henchmen who were always at his heels. From the docks the convoy would depart in glitter and fanfare across the highways, as it travelled to the secluded checkpoints, isolated in the woodlands far out of reach of the Law.

It was no idle talk that one December – years gone by – 350 tons of hard-core slabs of the commodity had penetrated the Venezuelan market. But this time, over-printed in red with Santa Claus on the claycoated boxes, the merchandise had infiltrated the hinterlands, across marsh lands to unmarked spots. There, access to the precious merchandise was by helicopters only, some even camouflaged in stippled green to look like police recon-naissance aircraft, the pilots garbed in blue, their tunics laden with brass buttons tight up to their thick moustaches and the pair of leggy blondes in fancy corduroy denims, adding an incongruous accessory to that deceptive aura of authority. The big chopper would descend with its whirr of blades blowing up the debris and dried sand all over the stacked bales whose overhanging straps would be looked up in one swoop as they cleared the shaggy tree tops and were deposited on another point along the route for distribution, by the highly organised, co-ordinating net-work of couriers. They came out of the jungles and abandoned mud-compacted runways, where the mari-juana would assume new names under the guise of food, medicines, machine parts, clothing with fictitious data on the bills of ladings, and on the packages found on the under carriages of vehicles, within the holds of vessels, lining the false bottoms of suitcases and best of all, concealed around the stomachs of attractive women travellers. They had the temerity to offer samples to the guards even in the presence of sniffing dogs. Then they would rely on their charms and seductive glamour for the exculpation of the crimes, whilst munching their crumpets Aided by Max Factor and Cartier, they paraded with their airs of specious charisma, whispered husky-toned into the guards' ears, their promises and more promises of love, and dinner dates, high in the penthouse swing clubs of the Sheratons.

There, overcome by the effervescent sparkle of Moet de Chandon they would soak in the dreamy music, dancing cheek to cheek, beneath glowing chandeliers, the hip hugging Dior creations swaying obsequiously to the music made alive by the jazzy staccato of muffled trumpets – renditions by Monk and Kenton, and the pulsating rhythm of South American swing of Prado. Then on to the porch under the canopy of pallescent stars where the whole city glittered and where they could unmistakedly point out almost with pinpricking accuracy the numerous buildings obliterating the city skyline built out of hashish money.

Here sat the corporation at its board meetings punctuated by loud expostulations. There was a nurtured complacence amongst its members whilst basking in the success of secret operations – the false fronts of location charts concealing the accounts, names and addresses of markets – worldwide markets that supported the growth of the corporation and its projects. The expanding claws of control that rapaciously outnumbered their rivals in the bid for supremacy steeped with greed that clouded the vision with megalomaniac callousness. The same greed that spawned the butchering of enemies and even patriots with a knowledge that they would be represented at the high courts before those corrupt judges who became emotional, who prejudged their cases at will. That husband and wife team of the syndicate that bribed and terrorised the jury with threats, extorted evidence from the peasants and then blackmailed them after the trials.

But there was not another event in the whole history of the organisation which demanded so much planning and bravado, so much cunning and painstaking secrecy, than that night when the select group peered over the abstruse drawing laid down on the boardroom table with the faces leaning over the rising smoke of cigars, discussing the proposals leading up to the plot of destroying the most important man in the organisation. The killing of Rodrigo Fernando Sanchez, president.

He was killed one night as he sat down in his penthouse office. News of his death, garbled through the intercom, hot in the wireless via coded messages, flashed through to the ranks of Gonzalez, Ramon, past Alcazar, filtering to Amlandoz and finally overseas into the fullerton high-woods to Saragun and Dole, by which time Cachipe, Bristol, and even Pahari, were alive with the news.

Yet, one month afterwards, he was seen still sitting, even more broad chested at his desk, with his swarthy smile. A little grey at the temples, the diamond studded hands and his head plastered, crowning twin spots of dark sunglasses.

King of the Carnival

Stooped in the darkness of his paper shack, Santo the Maskman spat through the doorway and yawned. Below him, way down the Hill, the city buzzed and came to its awakening like a huge leviathan, the streetlights dulled by the dawn that heralded the bands, Casablanca, Free French and Tokyo, and even Merry Makers, abandoning their camps that had smoked in the months of heat and fever until now. The hordes, the waves of dancing feet marched out, thronging the streets, clogging the freeways in thousands amidst the thunderous din of steel and tin and in some places, the shattering shards of glass and bottles.

So the war had started, the pitched battles begun between the bands, stirring the bitter dyes of animosity and hate. But those were the battles of the boys from the Hill, from across the River and further up district, from smaller panyards. He had his own private battleground elsewhere – in the savannah, beneath glaring stage lights that broke in shafts of lighted motes over the judges' heads.

And so he had trudged home, Santo, head bowed in defeat, humiliated, the aimless shuffle of feet, dragging, not knowing their way home over cobblestoned paths of broken twigs and dried leaves. Through the stench of dog droppings and the dank odour of clothes-washings stagnant and frothy settling in cold ravines. Up Piccadilly street with Basillon on the right and on the other side, streets steep and slippery, curving like Belgrade and Harpe Place. He wore a heart, as heavy as his shattered headpiece.

'They make the white man first and I not even placing,' he mused, sitting glum in the paltry confines of his paper throne, flimsy like the futile thoughts hovering over his weary head, as he gazed into the cityscape from the Hill. This Hill – the castle on his domain out of which skulkers and badjohns had emerged challenging and elusive as the chameleons that came down the star-apple tree clinging to the red barren rock; the snare and the snarl etched around their lips in defiance of the grit and poverty around them. Dust on his lips, in his throat, and, in his eyes, the fading alexia of the unschooled, of the untutored.

But the terrible pang was inside him. It had seized him as it had done these past twelve years, growing within him, gnawing his insides like a leech that came out of his hands as he fashioned and he carved and he etched in the glyphs and in the furrows of metal and leather, crafting the delicate beads nimbly in his hands, the silken gossamer webs spangled in fulgent iridescence of sparkle and wild fire. Wild too in his eyes, the pang had erupted in a fierceness no one understood. And they thought him a madman, a maniac stooped forever over the head of his dragon in its contemptible magnificence of horned-plated scales each lapping over in repeated clusters of copper and brass, bound and stitched together by his skill and the patience of long, flambeau-lighted nights and the terrible desire within him to bring home the prestigious crown of the King of Carnival.

So he stood now in his glory. Tall. Glittering. The thick

negroid arms. The massive thighs. And his shoulders,
Atlas-like, bearing the load over his head and around him
like his ancestors in the dim-lit forests of distant lands, or,
in reminiscing, like the more recent folks under maho-
gany and cacao in the quiet backwoods of our own land
where they toiled in the groves between panniers, always
toting like bachacs as if destined to all eternity in this task,
except that now the load on his shoulders gave him a
proud, urgent feeling of having created and conquered,
bringing out to the world the skill and genius of his people
made manifest by this huge prehistoric demon out of
legend and the mythical past in his portrayal that would not
only mesmerize and astound, but would also destroy the
fallacy in the minds of others that he and his kind had not
their places in the pews and podia of society.

So in the instrument of this terrible phantasm coming
out of its lair, rising from the scum and trodden
marshland, he laboured with love, ignoring sleep and pain
and forgetting hunger that was never gratified by the thin
pottage of ochro and dumplings he kept near his tin of
paste.

And now he sensed the triumphant feeling coming up
from the toes, from the claws, ascending along his spine to
his cranium as he edged centre stage, lifting the great
head of the beast sequined and fashioned to the uncanny
similitude of the mesozoic monster that crawled and
slithered with its flailing tail, spitting out fire, fuming over
the audience until they roared "Dat is mas". And mas' it
was. Captivating and panoplied as he stood in triumph on
stage before the thousands now on the edge of their seats.
He raised his elbows, pulled at the network of wires
strapped to his fingers inside the costume, manipulating

the great animal, turning its head, the front paws and the thrashing tail. The jaws opened blood red, eyes bulging in a rage to the tune and to the promise he had made as written on the programmes, that he was going to make the dragon dance, dance for them. So the pans mellowed and a hush prevailed, the master of ceremonies dragged the microphone cord out of the way and Santo, as he had done so many times before practising in his own back-yard, got on the hind legs of the reptile and shifted its weight from side to side, the sinuous body swaying with the music. The crowd laughed and yelled.

"Take dem, Santo," someone shouted from the side of the stage.

"He come good, man. Look at that thing, man must be spend he whole life behind it."

"You think he goh make."

A squeaky voice came from the back. "You tink it easy! Man does band dey jaw and belly, starve the whole year just for tonight."

"Look, dat is blood and sweat and long tears."

"Dat's why he wife leave him."

"Just for one night, eh boy?"

"Dat's it boy – only showing how we people could bare the grind."

"We have belly – guts. Recession or not."

"Guts? Talent!"

"You sure right!"

"How ah talk?"

"Brave, man, brave."

And Santo, peeping through the holes of his scaly costume, heard the approval of the audience, saw the nodding heads of the white-faced judges and, relishing the ovations, bowed and retreated, making room for the others to come on stage.

They too, danced in their glory, chipping away before the judges, covered with feathers and silk, bobbing and weaving in the gorgeous display of tinsel and paint and foil and lamé. For them the applause was loud, also, as each one paraded: Atilla the Hun, Genghis Khan, the copper toned Montezuma, Chief Great Hunting Bear, Waxatalabah burly as a bison under the brilliant canopy of mirrors, beads and white bones, his headpiece so large it tore down the overhead wires. But it was the last masquerader that caused him to turn his head as he rested backstage. It was the white man again – last year's winner. Santo recognized the walk, the delayed gait, the stooped shoulders, and immediately his forehead became cold beaded.

Now the white man moved on stage alone. But his costume was neither large or billowing. It lacked bulk, weight, without the pastiche of laboured details, taking up a smaller space. But its magnificence was in its modern, technological revelations. It came on stage, part man, part robot, its co-ordinating movements mechanized, the eyes sparked, it spoke, it buzzed, sang, emitting clouds of tinted smoke, a perfumed spray. Then from under it, wheels came out as they rolled across the stage, coloured lights appeared in clusters, brightening the whole stand in a strong incandescence, whirling around to the musical sounds coming out now from its mid section. And the crowd was stunned, taken aghast by the scientific display. Hysteria. It stood up before the antics of this masquerader, this new invention, his novel interpretation of mas.

So the second round of parade came one hour later,

when the judges had exchanged their score sheets with one another between drinks and the interval allowed fidgety movements between the seats of the audience enthralled by the last moving spectacle it had just witnessed.

And then the final moment arrived. All were to parade once more. Atilla the Hun appeared hoary, mustachioed, powerful in his gilded boar-skin cape, pelted pouches dangling at his side and the bronze epaullettes hugging his shoulders. King ABUBAKARI II the black Muslim looked ferocious, indigo-blue under the spotlight in leather trappings, filigreed coat, his broad silver shield embossed like his breast plate over which his yardbroom beard hung, unkempt, frazzled. Then his turn came. Once. Twice. His name was called – "Santo Lovelace and his dancing dragon."

But he just stood there silent and alone, among the stage hands, unmoving, leaning against his dragon, idle and grotesque, the heaving expanse of his chest now subsided, and beaded brow frowned to quietude. And in his eyes, the cold stares of the vanquished fanatic or genius, lost in some soporific trance in which sacrifice, devotion and long seasons of rehearsals were now laid waste.

He still heard his name being called through the microphone when he left, as he quietly pushed his dragon head low, through the flats on to the grass outside, and he never forgot the fearful vision of the white-faced judges, pencils on their lips, and the white masquerader prancing and jiving in his robot contraption under confetti and streamers, with his ostentatious performance and the popping noises, and the battery of lights that stuttered, exploding around him.

Glossary

Glossary of East Indian words

Aloo: potato
Backra: white man
Baggee: spinach
Beta: son
Blacksage: type of grass
Bon dong: burn down
Cacapool: bad quality
Calabash: gourd
Carat: broad palm leaves for covering, used to thatch houses when dried.
Chacha: uncle
Chachee: aunt
Chan: paddy rice
Channa: type of pea
Chataigne: name of fruit (tree)
Choka: paste made out of cooked vegetables
Chula: earthen fireside
Chupidness: stupidity
Creoni: creole
Dasheen: type of vegetable
Datwan: hibiscus stick used for scrubbing teeth
Doh: don't
Dougla: a person of mixed blood
Geera: type of seed used for seasoning
Gul: girl
Loce pok: roast pork
Mahoe: type of tree
Mamoo: uncle
Nannie: grandmother
Orhni: head veil
Panee away la: rain is coming
Primrose: type of yellow fragrant-fruit
Roti: flat round bake
Sada: plain roti without filling